AT B. A. T. T.

AT B.A.T.T.

by

Gershon Kranzler

Published and Copyrighted 1978 by

MERKOS L'INYONEI CHINUCH, Inc.

770 Eastern Parkway, Brooklyn, N.Y. 11213

5740   1980

Second Printing 5740-1980

ISBN 0-8266 — 0368-8

נדפס בדפוס האחים גרויס

Printed in U.S.A. GROSS BROS. Printing Co. Inc.

Table of Contents

AT B.A.T.T.

Bnei Abraham Talmud Torah, whose students are the heroes of these stories, is one of the many Hebrew schools which provided a basic Jewish education for Jewish youth in the period following World War II, before the Day School movement began to flourish.

B.A.T.T. is located in an old Brooklyn neighborhood near a newly built City Housing Project. The area provides a cross-section of many types of people, some of whom form the background for the stories which follow.

Directing the Talmud Torah is Rabbi Abraham Greenberg, a young Rabbi who is filled with dedication and devotion to Torah Judaism and able to inspire his students and transmit to them his ideals. He is devoted to his students, always ready to assist them not only in their studies, but also in their personal problems. He sets a fine example as a Torah scholar and an admirable human being concerned for the welfare of his fellow.

The students at B.A.T.T. are young Jewish boys who take their studies seriously, yet love adventure and excitement. Among them are Benny, the Talmid Chochom, the star student, the undisputed leader of the group; Yossi, the best athlete, usually Benny's right hand man in any project; Shloimele, the shy youngster; Yankie, the pessimist and critic; Melly, who starts out as the neighborhood tough guy; Ray Dorf, and many others who star in the adventures "At B.A.T.T."

The lot behind the Talmud Torah building serves as the exclusive meeting place for the boys. During recess, and after class, they gather there by the little wall to talk things over, to plan their exciting projects, and to cope with emergencies that frequently challenge life "At B.A.T.T."

The Unwanted Esrogim

You know what an Esrog is, don't you? It's the precious citrus fruit with the delicious fragrance over which a blessing is recited on Sukkos. Weeks before Sukkos, Jewish buyers start shopping around, wrapping and unwrapping the yellow citrus fruit from Eretz Yisroel or Italy or Greece, inspecting each for the tiniest defect in size, shape or color, as if the Esrog were a precious stone or rare metal. Prices vary from the low of twenty dollars to, as the dealers say, "The sky's the limit;" particularly in a year when the harvest is not plentiful.

But imagine the catastrophe when one year, during the Second World War, whole shiploads of Esrogim were stranded on the ocean, not able to get through the mine-infested waters. Many Jews had to remain without an Esrog, because they could not afford to purchase one of the few that did arrive on time.

A week after Sukkos, the boys of the Bnei Abraham Talmud Torah were discussing this turn of Divine Providence which deprived them of their own Esrog which they had had every year. Rabbi Greenberg, the principal of B.A.T.T., was fortunate enough to have an Esrog sent to him by the children of an orphan home in Jerusalem which the school generously supported. This Esrog was brought *in person* by a visitor from Eretz Yisroel! People offered Rabbi Greenberg as much as

9

two hundred dollars for it, but he would not consider selling it.

"I wonder what they'll do with all the shiploads of Esrogim that they unloaded in the harbor this week," wondered aloud Yossi, the school's star athlete.

"Well, they might just as well dump them all into the ocean," remarked Benny, the scholar of the Talmud Torah, and Yossi's best friend. "Now they're not worth a penny, unless a miracle happens, like the story the Rabbi told us. Remember? A poor Jew found a sack of Esrogim and sold it to the king whose daughter was very sick and nothing could cure her except Esrogim. So the king paid each fruit's weight in gold. I wish I knew of a way we could use those thousands of Esrogim which will just go to waste."

"The money sure would come in handy," said Yossi. "We could use it for a new building. Can you imagine a building with big windows and plenty of light and room to move?"

"Listen," Benny said. "Let's all give it some thought. Maybe someone will come up with an idea that can turn the unwanted fruits into a money-making enterprise."

Little Shloimele, as usual, asked a silly question. "But how are you going to get hold of the Esrogim, even if we can think of some scheme to make use of them?"

For a second, no one said anything. Shloimele smiled smugly.

But Benny blared out, "You little fool! They'll throw them at you for nothing, for the asking! You'll save them the job of carting the rotting Esrogim away."

The next day after class, the boys gathered at their favorite meeting place, the little wall behind the store where they studied until sufficient funds could be raised to acquire a proper building.

"Well boys," said Benny. He pushed his glasses up and squinted. "Have you thought of anything?"

There was not a single one among them who did not think that he had concocted a winning scheme. But upon closer examination, most of the ideas proved to be a sheer fantasy that would have done honor to Dick Tracy and similar heroes of the comics, but which could not turn belated Esrogim into a means of making money. One boy, for instance, suggested that they coat the fruits with gold and silver paint and beads and sell them as decorations for Jewish homes. Another proposed that they ask their mothers and sisters to cook the Esrogim and make them into jam and jelly that could be sold at a profit. A third suggested that they buy the Esrogim and store them in a freezer where they would stay fresh until the next year when they could sell them at a huge profit.

But as quickly as these proposals were made, they were discarded as impractical. Finally, only Yossi and Shloimele had not spoken, and all eyes turned to them.

"So what about you, Yossi," said Benny.

Yossi hesitated. "Well," he said, "I have an idea, but it needs some thinking through. Let Shloimele talk. Maybe by the time he is through, I'll have my idea worked out."

Shloimele blushed. He put his hands in his pockets and kicked at the wall. "I — I don't know if this will work, but I thought we could try to use what we learned in class about the Esrog, that it never loses its fragrance. I don't know how, but soda-makers or ice-cream manufacturers, or some other people like that might be interested."

That's it, that's it!" yelled Yossi. Everyone turned to look at him.

"I'm not kidding!" Yossi said. "Don't laugh. Shloimele gave me the idea I needed. My uncle has a place where they extract fruit juices and sell them. I read an article just the other day about the manufacture of soap. The author writes about the complaints of the soap manufacturers that many of the scents which they use don't last. By the time the soap is sold and used once or twice it has lost most of its pleasant scent. All we need to do is show a manufacturer that an Esrog never loses its fragrance. He'll buy these Esrogim right up! What do you boys think of that?"

"That's great!" "Hey, that's a terrific idea!"

"Just a minute," Benny said. "It is going to cost a nice bundle of money for anyone to carry out this idea. What manufacturer is going to want to experiment with 'Esrog soap,' the soap that will not lose its fragrance to the last bit," Benny laughed.

"No, no, no," the boys yelled. "We ought to try it. You can never tell."

Yossi, Shloimele and Benny got to work finding out how and where to get hold of the Esrogim. They asked Yossi's uncle about extracting the juice from the Esrogim and they wrote to companies to see who might be interested in their idea.

When they told Rabbi Greenberg about their idea, he was very skeptical.

"You need experts to handle such a thing," he said. "The executives of the big companies will not have time to see you."

"But Rabbi," Yossi said, "You always tell us that one can never tell what can come out of a bright idea."

Rabbi Greenberg laughed. "All right boys. Write to the companies and tell them you're representing B.A.T.T."

The boys took a quick trip down to the East Side and bought some beautiful Esrogim for a nickel apiece. Benny had an Esrog box which retained its strong scent from the preceding years. He thought it would be a good idea to show it to the manufacturers to prove the lasting quality of the Esrog fragrance.

They took several trips uptown and downtown to the offices of the famous soap manufacturers. No one liked the idea. "It is too expensive," one executive said. "I can't see you today," said another. No one would listen. The boys almost gave up the idea.

One day, the boys sat silently in the reception room of the most elegant office of the largest of all soap companies. Suddenly a relatively young man ran out of an inner office and rushed through the waiting-room where the three boys sat glumly, waiting for the secretary to find out whether someone would speak to them. Suddenly he saw the beautiful, old silver box which Benny had brought along. Curious, he stopped and walked over to the boys.

"What's this?" he asked, and smiled at them.

"An Esrog box," replied Benny, forgetting that not everybody in the world knows what an Esrog box is.

"What's that?" inquired the elegantly dressed young man.

"Here, smell it," said Benny and opened the beautiful old silver box which had been used by his grandfather and great-grandfather.

"Mm! This scent is wonderful!" the young man said "Come with me!"

The three boys followed him into his office marked "Office of the Vice-President."

Once they were seated in the large soft leather chairs around the young man's desk, Yossi explained his idea. The young man listened attentively to the boys all the while playing with the silver box, and occasionally taking a whiff of its fragrance, disregarding all the buzzing and ringing of the phones.

Yossi finished his story.

"Quite an ingenious idea," the young man said after a few minutes of silence. "But tell me, what would you do with all the money which you earn from the sale of this plan?"

Eagerly the boys explained to him the great importance of Jewish education for every Jewish child and described the high standard of their school, Bnei Abraham Talmud Torah, and the devotion of their principal, Rabbi Greenberg. They told of the great need for a building for their Synagogue and classrooms which served the entire neighborhood.

"Hmmhm," said the young man. "We might consider it. Let me have your address, and you will hear from me."

Two weeks later, a letter arrived at B.A.T.T. with a personal memorandum from the Vice-President of the large soap company to whom Benny and Yossi had spoken. He wrote that although the fragrance of the Esrog was superior to others used in soaps, it was, unfortunately, too expensive to extract the fragrance for use in soap. He wrote to Rabbi Greenberg how impressed he was by the sincerity of the boys and by their explanation of their love for their Jewish studies, and he sent a large check toward the construction of the Talmud Torah building in the Project as his personal contribution, and promised to raise the rest among his business associates.

"You see," said Shloimele proudly, "the Esrogim were good for something."

"You bet," agreed the other boys.

Half a year later, the Bnei Abraham Talmud Torah was able to move into its own building with bright classrooms and a good-sized Synagogue. The young Vice-President of the soap company accepted the honor of dedicating the building. The foundation-stone bore the engraving of an Esrog in an open Esrog-box, and the Synagogue became known as "Esrog Shul."

The Mystery of the Missing Druggist

There was great anxiety in the old Brooklyn neighborhood around B.A.T.T. The entire community of both Jewish and non-Jewish immigrant families from Poland, Ireland, Italy and Lithuania was concerned over the disappearance of Doc Alex Katz, or Old Doc, as most people affectionately called the druggist who owned the pharmacy a few blocks from B.A.T.T. As far back as anyone could remember, the old, slightly hunched druggist with the short grey beard and thick glasses had run his quaint drugstore as a humanitarian institution for anyone in need. No needy person ever walked out of his pharmacy empty-handed even if he was unable to pay for his medicine or for the essential needs for a baby's care. His prices were very low and he never charged more than he thought one could afford.

The boys from B.A.T.T. were his special favorites. He liked to ask them questions about their studies, rewarding them with delicious sour candyballs from the huge glass jar on the counter. In his youth, Old Doc had studied in a Cheder in Russia. He came to America after a pogrom in which his parents, as well as hundreds of other Jews, were brutally murdered. An uncle brought him out of Russia, raised and educated him. Old Doc never forgot what he had learned, and he was a real wizard in Jewish history. The room behind

16

his lab in back of the pharmacy was lined with hundreds of "Seforim" and other books. Since his wife had passed away many years before, these books kept him company until late into the night, as he studied at a table in the alcove of his library.

It was a rare night that people did not ring his loud night-bell with a request for an emergency prescription. He would then open the little window of the alcove, and ask:

"What can I do for you?" in his wheezy voice, which to people in urgent need sounded like a voice from heaven itself.

If the case warranted it, he would say, "Wait a minute. I'll be with you in a jiffy."

Needless to say, he was one of the most admired people in the entire neighborhood. And his name was famous far beyond it. Having an exceptional memory, he easily learned the languages of the people in the neighborhood well enough to communicate with anyone who sought his help.

It is understandable, then, why everyone was so worried when the news spread that Old Doc's drugstore had been closed for several days. Even when he used to go away occasionally, or on Shabbos and Holidays when the store was closed, people would leave their prescriptions in a large, iron mailbox near the front door of his store. Without fail, the prescriptions would be ready the next day, even if the old man had to stay up all night.

This time, however, it was different, and so very much unlike Old Doc. Also, there was an additional reason which gave cause for worry. A few months before, something very disturbing had happened to Old Doc that shocked the community. Hoodlums had broken into the drugstore one evening while Old Doc was preparing the prescriptions for the next day. They knocked him down, took all the money from the cash register, and ransacked the place looking for drugs. The pharmacist was in bed for several days, and it took some time before he was able to hobble around on crutches, and then with a cane. Against his will, neighbors began to patrol the corner in the evenings. Many drugstores in the area had closed up because of similar incidents, and Old Doc's pharmacy was not going to be touched again, if his neighbors could help it. To them the old, hunched druggist was a saint or maybe an angel in disguise.

The boys from B.A.T.T. used to take turns helping him in the early evening until he closed the store. The local police captain had a special alarm button installed behind the counter, and arranged that a police cruiser would never be far from the drugstore. The patrolmen on the beat would never forget to peek through the window to make sure their old friend — who always offered them a cup of hot coffee or a cold drink — was alright.

But now, the large mailbox was filled to the top with unfilled prescriptions. Neighbors gathered around the pharmacy discussing Old Doc's disappearance. One of them remarked that Old Doc had been seen in recent weeks carrying large bags filled with drugs, food and other items for people who were too sick or too proud to come to him for help. He had a whole network of scouts who would report to him if they learned of someone old, weak, or needy; and many a time he enlisted the help of his young friends from B.A.T.T. to help him carry the bags if they were too heavy — especially after the holdup.

Greatly worried, Benny and Yossi went to see Rabbi

Greenberg, when they heard that the old druggist had been absent for quite awhile. Rabbi Greenberg had a key to the drugstore, and so did Captain Duncan from the precinct. Rabbi Greenberg went with the policeman to check the pharmacy, but everything was in order.

The boys were discussing what might have happened and where they could find a lead to the whereabouts of their kind and learned friend, when Yankie suddenly shouted, "Hey guys, wait a minute! I do know something! Why didn't I think of it before?" He jumped up and slapped himself on the forehead in frustration. "I saw the old man just the other day. I was helping my father in his used furniture store. 'Hey, Yankie, look,' my father had said. 'There goes Doc Alex again dragging his shopping bags filled to the top. He used to come once a week or so, looking out for the old and weak who needed his personal attention. Lately, he is coming here more often.' By the time I had turned around, holding on to the heavy piece of furniture I was helping to fix, the old man had already disappeared around the corner and I could not let go of the furniture to run after him. How in the world did I ever forget about that, dumb-bell that I am!" Yankie exclaimed, slapping himself again on his forehead.

Yankie's father's store was located in an old Brooklyn neighborhood where there had once been many Synagogues and a rich Jewish life. But now, most of the Synagogues were either boarded up or converted to warehouses. And most of the Jews had moved away, except for the aged and poor.

The boys rushed to Rabbi Greenberg's office, relayed the latest piece of information, and asked whether they should go searching in that old neighborhood. Perhaps someone in the area would know the whereabouts of Old Doc. Rabbi Green-

berg transmitted this information to the police captain, who
assured the Rabbi that he and his men would do all they could
to trace Old Doc. He was not in favor of letting the boys go to
search for the druggist, but he finally agreed on condition that
they go only in groups, keep in contact with each other, and
never stay more than an hour.

The boys set out in three groups to search the old neighborhood. They took along the B.A.T.T. whistles which they had
bought after several boys got lost on a Lag B'Omer
trip. They used it only once on this search, when some
roughnecks started throwing stones at them. Within a short
while, all three groups joined together. Immediately, the roughnecks disappeared.

Before they left for the search, Rabbi Greenberg told
them, "On the way, check up on my old friend, Reverend
Silver. He lives behind the Greene Avenue Shul, where he
was Shammes for many years. When I lived in that neighborhood, he used to study Gemoroh with me when my father had
no time. When I last visited the Shul, it was almost totally
empty and badly damaged by neighborhood vandals. If he is
at home, he may have some idea where Old Doc may be."

The boys found many old, boarded up and vandalized
Synagogues during the few afternoons that they walked through
those streets.

"My father tells me," said Benny, "that there were large
libraries of 'Seforim' in each of these old Shuls. Early in the
morning, before going to work, and in the evenings, dozens of
Jews, many of them real scholars, would sit there and study
Torah individually or in groups."

"I wonder what happened to the 'Seforim' when the old

people moved or died?" said Yossi. "Did their children take their precious books along or just abandon them?"

"What a pity," said Shloimele, as they passed one of the old Synagogues that had been boarded up. Only a large Mogen David on top of the stone gable indicated that it had once been a Shul.

"Hey, watch out," yelled Benny, as they walked past the parking lot of a factory. Stones began to fly all around them from the broken windows of the factory. The boys from B.A.T.T. were determined not to get involved in any fights, so they quickly moved on. One of them noticed an iron Mogen David over a building right behind the fence of the parking lot. To the boys, all the streets looked alike — just long rows of dilapidated red or brownstone houses, their stoops, railings or fences falling apart.

"Benny, this is Greene Street," said Sammy. "See, there's the street sign. Perhaps that Mogen David belongs to the Shul which Rabbi Greenberg asked us to look up. Maybe his old friend, the Shammes, is there."

"You are right," replied Benny, when they stopped in front of the old, deep yellowed-grey brick building that was all boarded up, the windows covered with rusty iron grates. When the boys looked around, they noticed a heavy metal door in the back and a small dust-covered window high above it. Yossie thought he noticed a flicker of light through the window. So they decided to see if anyone was there. They knocked at the door, though they doubted if anyone would be living in a place like this, with rubbish piled up all around.

The door opened a bit. An old man peeked out. "Come in quickly boys," he said in a weak voice and closed the door quickly behind them. "I noticed your 'yarmulkehs'," he added, "so I let you in."

The boys entered a large, musty room that had once served as Beis Hamidrash, the study-hall of the Synagogue which was further up front.

"What are you doing here, boys? I haven't seen youngsters like you in here for quite a while," asked the old man.

"You aren't by any chance, Reverend Silver?" they asked.

The old man with the thin, white beard and large 'yarmulkeh' nodded in surprise. Benny told him about Rabbi Greenberg's request to look him up. Reverend Silver was very happy to hear about his young friend and about the wonderful work he was doing at B.A.T.T.

"How come you are still here? It does not look like there are many Jews in the area that would need a Shul with a Shammes?" asked Yossie.

"Where can I go? My wife and I are old, and we don't want to go into an Old Age Home. There are still quite a few old and poor people around here who gather here for a daily morning Minyan. Many others are sick and have stopped coming to Shul. If it were not for Old Doc Alex they might long ago have passed away for lack of proper care and medicine," he answered them.

"Why, you know Old Doc?" Benny asked. "He is the reason we are here. He has disappeared from the neighborhood where he lives without leaving a trace. Perhaps you can help us find him."

The old Shammes shook his head. "I have pleaded with him so often to be more careful of the wild kids that roam around in this neighborhood. But he still brings medicines for the sick people around here. Look what he has been up to recently."

Reverend Silver led the astonished boys into the small room behind the Beis Hamidrash. There were two old men mending torn and tattered Seforim. All the wall space was taken up by makeshift shelves, and empty cartons held additional piles of old and worn books.

"Old Doc Alex has been scouting the old Shuls and homes of the people he visits, looking for and collecting Seforim that haven't been used for years. There are literally hundreds of Chumoshim and even Gemorohs that are falling apart or rotting away in damp cellars or attics, eaten by dust and mildew. He pays the people, and they are glad to have the money and dispose of the books. Once a week he loads his finds into a taxi and brings the worn books here to be mended. The old men who do the work are only too glad to have something worthwhile to do with their time. He distributes the repaired books to Yeshivos or Shuls where people will use them."

"I wonder where he is now. Why doesn't he come home?" mused Benny.

As they were speaking, stones started to whistle through the air, hit the boarded up doors and windows and splinter the glass. A rough voice called out, "Get away, you little punks. Don't let me see you again attacking Old Doc's friends in here."

A moment later there was a knock at the back door.

"Open up, Reverend Silver. Old Doc sent me to you," a voice said.

The old man opened the door. A young fellow in work clothes came in and handed the old Shammes a note, adding,

"My friends and I will do our best to make sure that those nasty kids don't bother you any more. There is a taxi waiting for you outside. Old Doc told me to get it ready for you."

Reverend Silver read the note from the druggist aloud, "I am at the home of old Reb Menashe from Quincy Street. He and his wife are quite ill. We have been virtually under siege for over a week. Just today the man who brought you this note came to our rescue. Please come over right away. There is something we must take care of before we can bring the old couple to a hospital."

A few moments later, the taxi carrying Reverend Silver and the four boys from B.A.T.T. pulled up in front of the address on Quincy Street. Old Doc was looking out of the window from the top floor of the dilapidated rowhouse. When he saw the boys, his eyes sparkled with joy. He called to the old Shammes to stay downstairs with the taxi while the boys raced up the three flights of stairs. He embraced them and they told him about the worry his absence had caused and about their attempts to find him, which had led them to Reverend Silver just when his note was delivered.

It was indeed a strange story that the hunched druggist told the boys. "You see, old Reb Menashe here had not missed a morning Minyan until a severe fever struck him several weeks ago. A member of the Greene Street Shul told me about it. So, I decided to visit him. When I reached the second floor, a mean-looking man was standing there. 'Don't think you are going anywhere until that old man gives me what I want. I don't care if he starves to death, he's not leaving until I get it. Get in there and talk some sense into him!' The man waved a pistol into my face and ordered me to go on up. 'You better come down soon with the stuff or else,' he added. It took me quite a while to convince Reb Menashe that it was I and that it was safe to open the door. When I entered, Reb Menashe took me to the back room and without a word opened a closet. He pointed to several silver Torah crowns, silver shields and silver pointers that he had wrapped in cloths. 'That wild man must have observed me bringing them here after I saved them from the fire in the old Shul on the corner. Ever since, he has been watching my door, not allowing my wife to go out to buy food or medicine, and bothering me for the "loot".' Once I got inside, I couldn't leave either. I finally noticed one of my friends who works in a garage nearby pass outside the window. I called to him and warned him of the man with the pistol who was holding us prisoners. With the help of a few cops, he freed us and ran to bring Reverend Silver my message."

The boys carried the sacred Torah ornaments downstairs. The taxi took them, Reverend Silver, and the druggist to the Greene Street Shul. An ambulance was called to take Reb Menashe and his wife to the hospital.

Old Doc's arrival at his pharmacy was like the return of a hero. In a matter of minutes, the word of his discovery and his whereabouts spread. He refused to be interviewed by newspaper reporters; but he gladly accepted all the promises of help for his favorite projects to aid the poor and sick in the old Brooklyn neighborhood and to rescue the many hundreds of abandoned Seforim.

The Dreidel Contest

Aharon Yossel was a new student at the Bnei Abraham Talmud Torah. Like all new students, it was, at first, quite difficult for him to get accustomed to the many unfamiliar faces and ways of doing things at the school. If Aharon Yossel would have been just another boy from the Project, it would not have taken him very long to make this adjustment. Usually, after the first few days, any new student felt quite at home, especially since Rabbi Greenberg had taught his students all about the Mitzvah of welcoming a stranger into their midst.

But Aharon Yossel was a different story, as anyone who saw the boy with the long "peyes," the sad eyes in the thin face, and the obviously worn, threadbare kaftan and European cap would realize. When his father, a tall, gaunt man with a small beard, had brought him to school, he explained to Rabbi Greenberg that Aharon Yossel is not his own child by birth. He had found him in the concentration camp in Bergen Belsen, Germany, where his own father had died, leaving the child without anyone to care for him. He adopted Aharon Yossel and brought him and his own daughter to America not long ago.

When the boys of the Talmud Torah heard about the sad past of Aharon Yossel, they went out of their way to befriend him. But all their efforts were to no avail. Aharon Yossel remained shy and sad. To all their invitations to join them in play he answered, "Nein, ich ken nisht shpielen. (No I cannot play)."

He also refused to accept any of the clothes which they brought him from home. "Nein, ich vill nisht. (No. I do not want)," he would say, and shake his head sadly.

"You must have lots of patience with Aharon Yossel," Rabbi Greenberg explained to his students who were very sympathetic to the thin, pale boy. "He has experienced so many terrible things that even a grownup person would not be able to live through them and remain the same. Don't pressure him too much, but let him see that you do care about him."

In class he showed a great deal of interest and made rapid progress. Though he had not learned much before, he was soon in the highest Chumash class of the Talmud Torah, Class Daled. And even Benny, the Talmid Chochom of the class, had to concede that Aharon Yossel, although younger than he, knew his work at least as well as he, and beat him by far in translating into Yiddish. However, Benny was not at all jealous. He even went out of his way to point out to him that he, Aharon Yossel, knew more and was the best in the class despite the fact that he was the newest and youngest member of the class.

But after a while when the boy still did not respond, his classmates gradually stopped talking about him, and gave up inviting him to their homes or to join their games. They just let him go his own way. But then one day, Aharon Yossel came to school, his threadbare coat torn, his face all scratched, and even more pale than usual. Despite their sympathetic questions, he would not explain to his classmates what had happened to him. Next day he again bore the unmistakable marks of some violent struggle. The visor of his cap was half torn off and there was no mistaking that he had cried. But again he refused to say what had happened to him on the way to the Talmud Torah.

After class, Benny and Yossi went over to Rabbi Greenberg and asked him for Aharon Yossel's address. "It looks like someone beats him up on the way to school, and we want to see that it stops," they explained.

The next day, Benny, Yossi and Yankie waited patiently at the corner until Aharon Yossel emerged from his house. Just as they suspected, hardly had he reached the end of the block, when a group of ragged boys, roughnecks, with sticks and bats, started out after him, chanting, "Nein, nein, nit shlogen, nit shlogen. (No, no, do not fight)." One of them had put on a black coat, made himself "peyes" of wool and started to walk behind Aharon Yossel, imitating his every move to the great amusement of his companions.

"Wait a minute, give me your hat," he demanded and started to pull Aharon Yossel's cap off. The frightened boy kept on walking, holding tightly to his cap. From all sides, the roughnecks pulled at him and hit him until he was down on the ground.

At that moment, Benny, Yossi and Yankie charged in. With their fists flying, their eyes flashing, they yelled, "You rotten cowards," and fell on the attackers of their classmate.

Caught unaware, the gang of boys did not even put up a real fight. In a flash they were gone, leaving their sticks and bats behind.

"Don't you ever touch this boy again!" Yossi shouted

after them. Aharon Yossel had nothing to fear from his rowdy neighbors after this incident.

From that afternoon on, when the boys brought the pale, still trembling boy triumphantly to the Talmud Torah, he became one of the gang. He had learned that the friendship which all the students offered him, particularly the boys of class Daled, was sincere and not just curiosity or pity.

This incident occurred a few weeks before Chanukah. By the time this beautiful festival of light and joy ended, Aharon Yossel had become the hero of the Talmud Torah. It happened like this. Every year, Gimmel and Daled classes vied for the honor of Dreidel Contest Champion of B.A.T.T. They did not play Dreidel merely as a game of chance, but as a hot contest for the title of "Scholars of the School," played before the watchful eyes of the Board of Education, the Rabbis from the neighborhood, and the parents.

The class whose turn it was had to guess a Hebrew word that started with the letter Nun or Gimmel or Hey or Shin — the four letters inscribed on the Dreidel — on which the Dreidel had stopped. Knowing a word earned five points. Not knowing a word cost the team five points. Knowing a Scriptural verse that started with the word added five extra points. So, the Dreidel championship was quite a test of knowledge. And the five best students of each class prepared themselves for weeks for this event, looking up words and verses which begin with the four letters on the Dreidel.

Naturally, classes Aleph and Bais had little chance against the "scholars" of Gimmel and Daled. They were satisfied with a preliminary contest about the holiday itself. But then came the main event of the evening. Rabbi Greenberg gave the signal. The Gimmel team had the first chance to spin the huge

Dreidel whose letters were so big that the entire audience could see them. Things moved quickly in the first half hour of the contest. The boys were so well prepared that whatever letter came up, they had a word or verse ready. And if one team could not think of the right verse, the other team gained extra credit if they were able to fit a verse from the Chumash to the particular word.

But then things got tougher and slower moving. The Gimmel team, though younger in age, made up with excellent preparation what they lacked in scholarship. Quick on the draw, they beat the Daleds several times. But the words got harder and rarer, and both teams lost credit when they could not find words or passages within the time limit of one minute allotted to them.

Benny, Yankie and Aharon Yossel were on the team that was to defend the championship against the eager Gimmels. But as the younger boys were ready several times with a good answer, the sympathy of the audience swung over to them. Benny and his comrades were hard put to keep the score close.

Maximum playing time was one hour. There were five more minutes to go, and the score was ninety for the Gimmels to eighty-five for the Daled team. Each second counted heavily; both teams were sweating. Even the older experts who tried to outguess the bright students did not find it easy.

"Hay," shouted the crowd, when the Dreidel stopped.

It was Gimmel's turn. The seconds ticked away. They had used up practically all the words in the dictionary that start with "Hay," they thought. But at the last instant, David, a very bright youngster, came up with the word "Hovioh" and also with an appropriate verse, "Hovi'oh li tzayid v'asay li matamim," which they had learned in the story of Isaac's blessing.

"Hurray, David!" exclaimed the boys of Gimmel jubilantly.

When Rabbi Greenberg gave the signal to spin the Dreidel for the last time, there was dead silence in the large hall. One could hear a pin drop. Daled had only a desperate chance to draw, even if they could find a word and provide *two* verses. They had the very unlikely chance of still winning the contest by coming up with three verses.

The Dreidel spun. Then it slowed and came to a halt.

"Gimmel!" shouted the crowd before it had settled.

"Gozell," shouted Benny with sudden inspiration. And he himself had two verses because he remembered the section Mishpotim very well. But before the others could chime in, a hoarse cry from one of the boys of Gimmel went up.

"It's a 'Nun,' not a 'Gimmel'."

"We'll have to do it over," ruled Rabbi Greenberg.

Again the Dreidel spun, and strangely enough the Dreidel stopped again at "Nun." Tense silence settled over the crowd, the beads of sweat trickled down the Daled boys' brows. "Nun" was tough luck. They thought and thought, but no words, let alone verses, came to their minds. The seconds rolled on. Ten seconds to go. Eight seconds. Five . . .

"Nozir," shouted the rather thin voice of Aharon Yossel.

At once all five boys of the Daled team came up with a Scriptural verse. How could they forget. Not so long ago, in the portion Nosso, they had learned all about the Nozir and his sacred vows. They exclaimed three different verses.

Three verses indeed! In the last four seconds! They were the champions!

They carried Aharon Yossel on their shoulders in triumph off the stage and around the whole hall. He had won them the championship and averted shame from Daled. Aharon Yossel became the hero not only of their class but of the whole Talmud Torah.

The Chamisho Ossor B'shvat Forest

The students of the Bnei Abraham Talmud Torah were learning about Chamishoh Ossor B'shvat, the fifteenth of Shvat, the New Year of the Trees, and about the custom of planting seedlings in Eretz Yisroel on this day.

"I have an idea," said Benny, when the boys met outside after class. "Let's plan a program, something special, and send the proceeds from it to Israel for the planting of a small forest in a religious Kibbutz in the name of our Talmud Torah."

"Good idea," said Yossi, "but don't you think you are overestimating us a little? How much do you figure we'll have to raise even for a small forest?"

"I read in the newspaper that the planting of a tree costs about $3.00. And I figured that two hundred trees, two trees for each student of the Talmud Torah, would not be too much."

"Well, wizard, how in the world do you expect to raise $600? Six hundred, mind you, not six dollars or sixty?" asked Yankie.

"Right now, I can't give you the answer. But it seems to me that with something really exciting and dramatic it should not be too difficult for us to raise that sum," answered Benny confidently.

"OK genius, we are waiting for the bright idea. It better be a real good one that will open people's hearts and pockets," said Sammy.

The boys realized the value of Benny's suggestion and tried their very best to think of ways and means of raising the sum of $600 — a sum which was far more than anyone of them had ever seen. Most of them could not even imagine how much it really was.

But in the end, Benny and Yossi, always the leaders in any project of the B.A.T.T. students, came up with something that seemed worth trying. They were used to selling raffles, making pushke collections and similar projects. But they had never undertaken to run a bazaar by themselves. Well, that is exactly what Benny and Yossi proposed to their fellow students — and not an ordinary bazaar, just like any old bazaar run by the ladies auxiliaries in the neighborhood.

The last time the Werner circus was in New York, Benny and Yossi had spoken to the manager. They had admired the huge tent and the manager told them that this was a new tent which had just been purchased because the old one was not large enough.

"If we could somehow get hold of the old circus tent and bring some famous artists down some afternoon to sell and auction off the goods which we'll collect, I bet we won't have much difficulty in raising the money for the Chamisho Ossor Forest Fund," said Yossi.

"Of course, it won't be easy to get famous people to come down for the bazaar of a neighborhood Talmud Torah. Yet, I think it might be worth trying. One can never tell," Benny concluded enthusiastically.

But it was easier said than done. In the first place, how would they convince the circus owner to trust them with a tent worth several thousand dollars? And if he did, where would they put it up?

The circus was then performing in Long Island. So, on a Sunday afternoon, when they had no school, Benny and Yossi invested their whole week's allowance for a ticket on the Long Island Railroad, and travelled out to the circus. While the performance was going on in the big top, they sought out the manager who had told them about the discarded smaller tent.

When he heard their request, the burly old man started to laugh. "Do you know how much such a tent costs? Several thousand dollars!" he informed them.

"Well, I think if you lend it to us for one afternoon it might give you a great deal of publicity. While if you let it lie in storage, you don't get anything out of it," argued Benny.

"What kind of publicity are you thinking of?" asked the circus manager, his curiousity aroused by the idea of the naive, but sincere youngsters of B.A.T.T.

"I have an idea that we might get on radio and television to acquaint people with our project. And we'll of course, advertise that you lent us your circus tent for the day," said Yossi.

"OK son, when you let me know and I see you boys on TV for the first time you can count on me that I'll have my own people deliver the old tent to you and put it up where we were last year, in your neighborhood," promised the circus manager.

"Can we count on it?" asked Benny hopefully.

"Shake hands on it," replied the manager and offered his huge hand to the two boys.

B.A.T.T. was humming with excitement when the boys brought back the favorable report. Now the question was how to get on TV and radio. Every minute on TV cost a lot of money, as they found out when they called the National Broadcasting Company.

"Wait a minute," exclaimed Yossi, as they pondered the problem of how to get on TV without having to pay for it. "The man never said that we need an entire program of our own. I think it'll be sufficient if we try to get on a Quiz show like 'You Tell us' or some other audience participation program. If all of us in the Talmud Torah write letters to the station, I am sure we'll get some response."

A hundred notes of plea for a chance for the two boys to appear on the TV program did make an impression on the program director of "You Tell Us," the weekly junior quiz show, and he sent two guest tickets to them. Naturally the boys immediately called the circus manager and told him to be sure and tune in on the program.

Benny, the scholar of B.A.T.T. knew his Bible inside out. And Yossi was as well informed about baseball players as any boy his age in the United States. So, when they chose these two categories in the quiz show, they really outshone all other contestants. The result of their performance was much better than they could possibly have hoped for. The unusual intelligence of the boys and their perfect answers aroused the interest of the quizmaster, John Dunn, and he questioned the two boys about the letters B.A.T.T. on their sweatshirts and caps. In no time, he got the whole story of the project, and of the challenge of the circus manager to the boys. Being a real showman, he knew how to make a big "spiel" out of the curious story of the B.A.T.T. forest that was sure to touch the many thousands of listeners.

"Count on me boys," he assured them. "I'll get you some big name talent for your giant bazaar."

A telephone call from the circus manager was awaiting them when they walked out of the broadcasting studio. "You sure kept your word, boys. The publicity you gave me today alone is worth the trouble. Just set the date, and I'll have my people put up our old tent for you."

They were even more surprised when the mail brought many hundreds of letters from listeners to the TV program. Some sent in donations for the forest, others requested tickets, and still others offered merchandise for the bazaar.

Everything seemed to be coming along fine. Through John Dunn, the quizmaster, they came in contact with several famous TV stars and some of them accepted the invitation of the boys to participate in their show.

One day, a letter arrived that threatened to spoil the entire project. It stated that union members are prohibited to participate in an amateur affair like the B.A.T.T. Bazaar. They called the union boss, but he was a tough man and refused to yield to the pleas of the boys.

For once the boys of the Talmud Torah were at a loss for a solution. In their distress, they turned to the principal, Rabbi Greenberg, who naturally had just as little contact with unions and artists as they. He advised them to call the quizmaster; he surely would know how to handle such a problem.

So, when Benny told John Dunn about their problem with the union, he said, "Let me talk to the boss. Maybe if we

offer a percentage to the pension fund of the union as their
fee, he'll reconsider and grant permission for the stars to perform at your affair."

A few persuasive words from Dunn, as well as the offer
of a ten per cent share of the profit to the pension fund,
changed the mind of the union official, and he agreed to allow
the stars to perform at the Bazaar.

Once this problem was solved, the rest was a cinch — at
least so the boys thought, up until the last week before the big
affair. Things moved rather quickly. With the assistance of
one of the boys' father, who was a lawyer, they got permission
from the city to erect the big tent. The quizmaster of the TV
program arranged for Benny and Yossi to meet several of the
big name stars who would draw a crowd. Not all of them
could or would accept, but the few who did were well-known.
Through the parents who had business connections, the boys
were able to gather all kinds of merchandise. The word of the
big event got around. Large posters all over the neighborhood
announced the B.A.T.T. Bazaar, and tickets sold like hotcakes.

But then the unexpected happened, and it hit the boys
like lightning. The curious thing was that it came from their
own beloved teacher, Rabbi Greenberg. One day after class
when the boys were busily rushing out to take care of some
details for the big bazaar, Rabbi Greenberg asked Benny and
Yossi to come into his office for a moment.

"I have something very important to discuss with you."
"Look, boys," he said after a few seconds had elapsed and
during which they realized that something unusual and
troubling must be in the mind of their teacher. "I know how
much this affair means to you and how much work has gone
into it. But there is one thing I have to watch out for, and that

is the spirit and the reputation of the Talmud Torah. You see, in your zeal to carry out your project you have forgotten to check with me about the program. Many radio and TV personalities do things and act in some ways which we people of the Torah cannot accept. Some of the stars that were nice enough to volunteer their services are singers and dancers who earned their fame on the stage. But I don't think our Talmud Torah should promote them, or even have its name associated with them."

"But, Rabbi, I have seen these names in affairs for other Jewish organizations and institutions," Yossi remarked after the first few seconds of shock had passed.

"That could very well be," said Rabbi Greenberg. "It is good publicity for these stars to appear at charity affairs and they probably are good-natured and want to help worthy causes. But we as an institution of Torah learning must be more careful. You understand that, don't you?"

The boys did understand. "But what shall we do now," they asked in confusion.

"Well, boys, we have to find a way of eliminating those stars whose names would be inappropriate for us, even for such a worthy cause as your Chamisho Ossor project.

"But you cannot insult them by telling them that outright," worried Benny.

"That is true," agreed Rabbi Greenberg. "If necessary we'll cancel the whole project rather than go through with it in a way that is contrary to the spirit of Torah."

For two days the whole works stopped, and the boys were going around all upset. They had sold so many tickets.

They put in so much effort and energy to get things done, and now all would be in vain.

But as unexpectedly as the problem had arisen, came the solution. A big snowstorm buried the old Big Top and the streets of the city knee-high in snow, and the bazaar had to be postponed. Only those famous people whose names would not throw any adverse reflection on the spirit of the Talmud Torah were invited for the delayed opening of the bazaar.

Since the people realized the good purpose of this affair, they did not mind a shorter program and the absence of some stars, and they attended the bazaar in full force.

When it was all over, the boys of the Bnei Abraham Talmud Torah had a profit of close to a thousand dollars from the admission and the sale of the merchandise. A few weeks after the money had been sent to Israel, they received pictures of the young "Yaár Bnei Avraham" which adorn the walls of the Talmud Torah in remembrance of the exciting project and the hard work the B.A.T.T. boys had put into it to make it a success.

The Playground

"How mean!" "What a dirty trick!" shouted the students of the Bnei Abraham Talmud Torah in the Housing Project.

They were hurling protests and derogatory remarks against the man who had chased them off the lot behind the Talmud Torah and was busily knocking large iron spikes into the ground while a large roll of thin-meshed wire-net was lying nearby ready to be put up between them. There was no doubt in anyone's mind that fencing off the lot meant the end of the best part of the afternoon when the various classes played baseball against each other — Class Aleph against Class Bet, and Gimmel. against Daled. Daled always won the championship because Yossi, the best pitcher in the Talmud Torah, was on their team. His learning did not match his enthusiasm for sports, and Rabbi Greenberg had to exert special effort to make Yossi pay attention to his studies instead of thinking of the Dodgers, Giants, and Yankees, and daydreaming about which of the three he would join when he grew up. But once classes were over, Yossi was the hero of the playground on the lot behind the Talmud Torah, and the boys of the Aleph class proudly carried his glove for him, or held his Chumash and notebook while he pitched his knuckleballs and curves against the sluggers of Gimmel and his fast balls past the base-stealers of the Bet class.

But apparently all that was going to end now. Yossi felt especially deprived. The lot was his particular domain, and he considered it a personal insult when the man chased them off and informed them that the owner of the lot would no longer permit the students of B.A.T.T. to use it as a playground.

"We have a 'Chazokoh'," shouted Benny, the "Talmid Chochom" (scholar) of the Talmud Torah, who learned Gemoro and knew that if a person occupies a piece of land for three years without anyone claiming ownership, the land belongs to him. But apparently the man who was putting up the wire-netting had never heard of a "Chazokoh."

"Let's have a war-council," said Yossi, after all the shouting and protesting did not prevent the man from fencing off the lot that meant so much to them.

"We must do something about this," he said when they all had arranged themselves on the small wall behind the Talmud Torah.

"What can we do?" asked the timid kid-brother of Yossi.

"Be quiet, kid," replied his big brother. "Not everybody is so chicken-hearted. We are a hundred guys."

"*Kein yirbu* (may they increase)," interjected Benny remembering what Rabbi Greenberg had taught them.

"We are a hundred guys, *kein yirbu*," continued Yossi unperturbed. "We can surely do something if we work together. Let's spend an hour after our classes are over picketing this lot. We'll make large signs and walk up and down in front of the fence, just as the workers did when they went on strike against the owner of the cafeteria across the street. All the people of the housing project as well as the passing pedestrians will see our sign. I bet you, we'll see some action soon!"

Benny protested. He felt it was not right to take such drastic action. "Perhaps a delegation of our students should go to see the owner and try to persuade him to donate the lot to the Talmud Torah."

But all the others disagreed with Benny. They preferred Yossi's protest to Benny's attempts at peaceful persuasion.

"What chance do we have of persuading the rich but stingy Sam Sperber, president of Sperber Realty Company, to donate the lot to the Talmud Torah?" argued Sammy, the oldest boy of Bnei Abraham. His father was one of the members of the Project Association and he always heard him talk about the heartless Sam Sperber who owned the lots around the Project, and gave the people of the Project a great deal of trouble.

"Let's have a vote," demanded Yossi.

As expected, the majority was in favor of forming a picket line around the fenced off lot. Even Benny was no longer so sure that his proposal was a sound one. But he managed to convince them to consult with Rabbi Greenberg before they go out protesting. Yossi was not keen on this idea because he was afraid Rabbi Greenberg might object to his plan. However, since all the other boys agreed that this was the proper thing to do, he consented to accompany Benny and present the issue to their Rabbi.

Rabbi Greenberg, who always refereed the baseball finals and had himself been one of the best sluggers of his Yeshivah team, knew just how his boys felt and sympathized with their plight. He told them that officially he could not give his permission for a protest. However, if the students wanted to do something like that on their own . . .

So it was decided to picket the lot to bring their plight to the attention of the neighbors.

"My father is a sign painter," said one of the boys. "He'll make us the signs."

"I know where we can find a lot of sticks just the right size," volunteered another.

Yossi was nominated to direct the campaign and he planned everything carefully.

The picketing of the Talmud Torah students against the owner of the Sam Sperber Realty Corporation was big news in the entire Project. Even some of the non-Jewish youngsters in the Project volunteered to join and help carry the large signs that read: "We, the students of the Bnei Abraham Talmud Torah, protest against the man who is depriving us of our playground."

A local newspaper sent a reporter and a photographer to the scene. There was lots of excitement. Yossi felt like a real big shot, giving interviews and explaining their cause. Rabbi Greenberg assumed responsibility for his students' action, though he said it was their own idea, and he felt that they were right in protesting against such an injustice, for there was little use being made of that dirt-littered lot behind the Talmud Torah.

On the third day of the protest, a big, shiny Cadillac drove up to the lot. Mr. Sam Sperber, the rich, old man who owned the lot, accompanied by two policemen stepped out of his car and said, "I am ashamed of you Jewish children. Don't you know better than to demand things which don't belong to you! Instead of being grateful that I let you use the lot all this time, without getting a penny for it, you make unreasonable demands. That is disgraceful for students of a Talmud Torah. I say, children, get away from here, or the police will take care of you. If I hear about any more stunts like this, I'll evict your Talmud Torah from my property."

Yossi and most of the other boys were eager to go on with the protest. Even some of the parents were ready to support the cause of their children. But Rabbi Greenberg explained to his students that force was not the Jewish way. Instead, he suggested that the students and their parents get together and find some way to finance the purchase of a lot for a playground, or at least raise enough money to rent one. This settled the matter temporarily and the tumult abated.

All this happened just two weeks before Purim. The afternoon after the protest was called off, the children were heatedly discussing Mr. Sperber's insensitivity. Rabbi Greenberg explained to them that Sam Sperber was a bitter, old man who had no children or family, and they should not condemn him too harshly.

"He just does not know better. Had he studied in a Talmud Torah, he might have known more about charity and kindness and its rewards. You all think that he is rich because he has so much money and owns so many buildings and has a big, shiny Cadillac. I tell you, he is really a very, very poor, old man . . ."

These words, of Rabbi Greenberg made a deep impression on the boys at B.A.T.T., particularly on Benny. He gave it much thought. The following week when they discussed the laws of Purim, an idea came to his mind. He talked to Yossi, and on Purim morning the two, the best baseball pitcher and the best student of Bnei Abraham, went uptown together, to one of the tallest skyscrapers, carrying a large, round package.

"Sperber Realty Corporation," read the gold-lettered inscription on a beautiful office door on the thirty-fifth floor of the building.

"Wait a moment," said the secretary when the boys told her that they wanted to give something to Mr. Sperber. After some time, she opened the door leading into the inner office of the luxurious suite. "Mr. Sperber is very busy, but if you can make it very fast you may go in for just a moment."

Another door opened, and Benny and Yossi found themselves in a room that seemed to have been cut right out of a magazine. Mr. Sperber, too busy to look up from the stack of papers on which he was working, said in his harsh voice, "What do you kids want? I'm a busy man. Don't waste my time."

Yossi, usually as courageous as any pitcher on the sandlot, was trembling. But Benny grabbed the package and stepped forward to the desk. "The students of the Bnei Abraham Talmud Torah send you *Shallach Monos.*"

"Ah, you are those fresh kids from the Jewish school who picketed me. What is it this time?"

"We have brought you a Purim gift. Our Rabbi explained to us that you are really not so bad; that you have no children and family and have experienced little kindness in your life. Today is Purim and we Jews send gifts of food to our fellow Jews. And we students of the Talmud Torah thought that you are really an unhappy man and our *Shallach Monos* would make you feel good."

Mr. Sperber's face turned very red, redder than a beet. But then he became pale and his face lost its angry expression. A few long minutes of silence passed. Then Mr. Sperber turned his face back down to the papers on which he had been working. The boys thought it was a sign for them to leave. But Mr. Sperber rose, walked around to the front of his desk, put his arms around the shoulders of the two boys and said:

"I thank you, boys. Perhaps your Rabbi was not so wrong. This is indeed the first sign of kindness I have experienced in a long time. I thank you for the Purim gift. I remember when I was your age and I lived in the old country, my mother used to send me out to her friends and acquaintances with the *Shallach Monos*. I, too, have a little *Shallach Monos* I want you to take back to your Rabbi."

He drew a piece of paper from the file cabinet behind his desk and handed it to Benny. "This is the title to the lot behind the Talmud Torah. Here. It's yours for good. I'll pay for having it fixed up into a splendid playground."

The students of the Bnei Abraham Talmud Torah celebrated the opening of the new playground and Mr. Sam Sperber was the guest of honor at that joyous occasion. The old man also became the chairman of the board of directors of B.A.T.T.

And that is how, through the mitzvah of *Shallach Monos*, by giving an old, embittered man the opportunity to share in the joy of the holiday of Purim, the boys of B.A.T.T. acquired their own playground.

The Shushan Show

The annual Purim party was always the main event in the calendar of the students of the Bnei Abraham Talmud Torah. The whole Project was looking forward to the happy celebration, for all Jews, old and young, were invited to attend and share in the fun and festivities.

The week after the Chanukah festival ended, the boys of the Talmud Torah got together to elect the Purim Marshal and to plan the program which they hoped would excell and surpass all previous ones.

Nobody was surprised when Benny was elected Purim Marshal that year. Yossi had been Marshal the previous year and had done a fantastic job.

"The only one who could top Yossi," said Shloimele, the youngest member of the Talmud Torah, blushing as he spoke, because everybody looked at him, "is Benny. He is our 'Talmid Chochom,' and he always has good ideas."

For the last time, Yossi swung the candy-striped baton ceremoniously and handed it over to the Marshal-elect. "To the new ruler of Shushan with my compliments and best wishes for even greater success than I had," intoned Yossi.

Immediately, everyone was showering Benny with suggestions to make this coming Purim Party the best ever. Benny listened politely to the brilliant ideas of a larger carnival, a bigger parade through the length and width of the Project, and a show of shows the likes of which even Broadway had never seen. And then Benny rose to make his acceptance speech.

"I am very grateful to you, Chaverim, that you have given me this great honor, and I shall try my very best to fulfill the expectations which you all have for me. I know that it will be practically impossible to do a better job than my worthy predecessor did last Purim. But I hope, with your cooperation, to find a way of making this year's party a memorable one."

"The suggestions that you have all given are very good ones — but I had hoped we could come up with a really new kind of program. I would say that we should study the story of Purim well, and perhaps from the Megillah itself we can get some inspiration on how to make this party unique. Let's meet again next week or even in two weeks, and see if anyone comes up with a new idea."

As usual, Benny had his way. The boys of the Talmud Torah knew they could depend on him. Meanwhile, they got busy to select a finance committee to raise the funds, a committee for refreshments, and the other arrangement committees that make a party a success.

One week passed, then another. The boys got together, but no one, not even Benny himself, had a really good or novel idea. They studied the Megillah thoroughly, but no new ideas emerged.

Then one afternoon, Rabbi Greenberg, the beloved principal of B.A.T.T., sent Benny on a special errand. When

Benny returned, he was all excited. Immediately he passed the word around that all the boys should meet at their favorite place, the little wall behind the Talmud Torah building, for a special meeting.

Everyone was excited. Benny had hit on something big. That much was obvious. After the classes were over, all the students gathered quickly, and in much less time than usual they were quiet, looking at Benny expectantly.

But they waited in vain to satisfy their curiousity. All Benny would say was: "I have a wonderful idea for a really great Purim party. What, when, and how, I cannot tell you or else it will lose its whole thrill. So I want you all to have faith in me and prepare the party as if it were to be held in the usual way. Get gifts, cakes, candies, soda, prepare some funny plays and other kinds of entertainment. But everything else must remain a secret."

"But what about all our neighbors and friends who look forward to share our party as usual in the auditorium?" asked Yossi doubtfully.

"Well, to them, too, we shall advertise it as the 'Surprise Purim Party,' to be held in Shushan, exact location to be disclosed at the party. Tickets will admit them to the school here. And from here they will find out. I am sure they will trust us," answered Benny.

Not only did the people of the Project trust the children of B.A.T.T., but somehow word of their secret Purim party spread, and out of curiosity many more bought tickets than ever before. Donations of funds, cakes, cookies, candies, and gifts of all sorts poured in. The boys themselves, who at first had been a bit skeptical at the secrecy of the preparations, caught the spirit and did their utmost to help Benny. The Marshal himself seemed possessed of inexhaustible energy and novel ideas. Every day he came with another project to make the Purim Party more exciting, and to give each and every one of the students of the Talmud Torah an important task so that no one felt that he was left out. But only Rabbi Greenberg and Benny knew the details of the party.

And then, for a few anxious days, complications set in. It all started when Yankel did not get the coveted role of Mordechai in the "Purim Shpiel." You see, Yankel was not just another student of B.A.T.T. Next to Benny, he was the outstanding student and quite a few of the younger boys looked up to him as their leader. So when lots were drawn for the parts of the Purim Shpiel, and Yankel found himself with the role of Charvona who, though vital to the story, is only a minor character in the Megillah, he felt slighted.

"Lots are lots," commented Yossi, when Yankel turned to him with his complaint, for Yossi was in charge of the Purim Shpiel. "Better luck next time."

Everybody knew that Yossi was Benny's best friend. And so Yankel felt that somehow he was not given the proper consideration by the leaders of the Purim party. He began whispering to David, his best friend. Later, after classes were over, David gathered the clique of Yankel's friends and Yankel spoke to them.

"I think this whole thing of the secret Purim Party is a big hoax. And we are fools to let Benny and Yossi put it over on us and on all the people of the Project who buy tickets because they expect something from us. Now it's still time to stop the whole thing before it is too late and we are made the object of ridicule."

This kind of talk impressed the boys who did not have such a fancy vocabulary as Yankel, and the next day they demanded a special meeting of the boys of the Talmud Torah. Again, Yankel delivered his speech attacking Benny, Yossi, and the other leaders for making fools of the whole school and the neighborhood.

"Not only do I think this is an insult to all of us and to our intelligence," asserted Yankel, "but the name of our school is at stake. The whole Project is buzzing with excitement over the secret Purim party. If it turns out to be a flop, we won't be able to show our faces, and what's more, we'll lose the confidence of the people for all future projects. I propose that we now vote to ask Benny to reveal to us all about the Purim party. If not, we'll have to cancel it and go back to our good, old kind of affairs, when everybody knows what he is working for, instead of being treated like small children."

Benny turned pale when Yankel spoke. And Yossi was ready to start a fight right then and there, that is how enraged he was. But Benny stopped him.

"Let's have a vote and see how you all feel about this argument of Yankel's," he suggested.

Naturally, only the handful of his best friends dared to vote in favor of Yankel's proposal. The rest of the boys, and they were the majority, expressed their confidence in Benny.

"You can out-vote me here," said Yankel, "but you cannot make the people of the Project fall for your hoax. Only today Mr. Liebowitz, the owner of the bakery, said that he would cancel his whole donation of cakes unless he knew what the stuff was going for. And what Liebowitz does, all the others will do. I kind of hate to think how our party will look without their donations."

At that moment Rabbi Greenberg happened to pass by and he overheard the angry remarks of Yankel. He stopped, turned to the boys and told them. "You can tell Liebowitz and the others whose donations we get that I guarantee for this party. They have no reason for alarm. We have never yet let them down. And I assure you, you and they can have the fullest trust in your Marshal."

Well, that ended the rebellion once and for all.

Finally, the big day came and the Talmud Torah auditorium was filled with food, sweets and other things necessary for the party. It was a Sunday afternoon; everyone who had a ticket came on time. At 2:00 P.M., four large buses rolled around. They were decorated with streamers and posters wishing all a Happy Purim and a Bon Voyage on the trip to Shushan. For half an hour the buses drove all over town, and then they finally came back into the neighborhood of the Talmud Torah. Squeals of joy and shouts of surprise from the happy children filled the buses. But when no one expected it, the four large vehicles came to a halt just a few blocks from the Talmud Torah, in front of the large Bikur Cholim Hospital and Old Age Home.

The boys and their audience could not believe their eyes. A huge sign over the entrance welcomed them to Shushan. Benny stood in front of the building, in the Purim Marshal's uniform, and a band was grouped behind him.

"Line up for the Purim procession," he commanded.

And then began the strangest parade. They marched through the long, gloomy hospital halls, singing, playing their instruments, picking up old men and women in the wheel chairs and taking them along from one wing of the huge building to the other, and then out into the large garden behind the hospital. Each of the boys pushed a wheelchair. And it was hard to decide who had more fun, the old people in the wheelchairs, or the boys who pushed them.

In the large clearing in the center of the garden were many rows of chairs for those who were able to walk there on their own, and who now waited expectantly for the big surprise. The boys and their guests spilled all over the lawns, sitting on the benches placed in a huge circle around the old people and patients in wheelchairs and on the grass. Fortunately Purim occurred quite late in the year and it was a beautiful spring day. The Purim Show was never as inspiring and well-played. The gifts never seemed to be so appropriate, as when each of the boys gave something to a patient or an old man or woman in a wheelchair. The auctions, the fun, the clowning and happy singing had never been as enjoyable as when the worn and weary expressions changed to smiles of joy and happiness, showing that they had a wonderful time, a real Purim treat.

Before the final Shushan Parade began to make its way through the huge hospital complex, from floor to floor, young boys, old men and women and their huge, happy audience, led by Benny and the enthusiastic band, one of the old people in a wheelchair, with a flowing white beard, said a few words of appreciation.

"I don't think you boys realize what this Purim Surprise means to all of us who sit amid the same four walls, day after day, with hardly anyone to talk to or any other topic of conversation except our illnesses and ailments and who died yesterday. Never in your whole lives will you be able to do the mitzvah of 'Mishloach Monos ish l'rai'ai-hu' in a more worthy and proper manner. Your spirit is the spirit of Morde-chai and Esther, who were concerned about their people more than their own lives. May G-d bless you all for what you have done for us."

Neither the boys nor the audience doubted that this had been the nicest and happiest Purim Party they had ever cele-brated. And the boys all pledged not only to come back to the hospital the following year to share their fun with those who have so little joy left in their lives, but very often during the year just to visit the patients and give them some "nachas" from Jewish Talmud Torah students.

The Surprise Party

A flurry of excitement passed through the classes of the Bnei Abraham Talmud Torah.

"Did you see the new student?" the youngsters from the lower classes asked each other. The older ones discussed his impudence, his chutzpah, when his father brought him into the classroom.

"Remember, Rabbi," he said defiantly. "I am coming here because my father is forcing me to. I have no interest in Hebrew. I do not wish to go to school here and I'll make every effort to get out of here as quickly as possible. You'll soon be glad to get rid of me. Just because my father studied Hebrew when he was young doesn't mean I must do it too."

When the boy finished talking, the students were in for a big surprise. Rabbi Greenberg who never permitted them to bet, said to him, "You wanna bet?"

That was all Rabbi Greenberg said. Taken by surprise the boy flushed and got all flustered. He hadn't expected this kind of reaction. He shook Rabbi Greenberg's hand, and although he kept his defiant scowl, he willingly went to his seat, chosen by Rabbi Greenberg — the seat next to Yossi, the star athlete of B.A.T.T.

"Hi, my name is Yossi Newman; what is yours?" asked Yossi.

"Roy Dorf," he answered shortly. "And don't bother about being pals. I am not here to stay."

That ended the conversation for the time being. The lesson continued as if nothing had happened and no one, not even Rabbi Greenberg, commented when the new boy occupied himself with shooting spitballs at the flies that crawled on the window.

During recess, the boys played handball.

"Challenge," said Yossi to Roy as he left the classroom after the rest of the class.

"Challenge yourself," he replied curtly, but sat down and watched furtively as Yossi and Benny engaged in their usual contest.

"You hold your hand too straight when you hit the ball," Roy remarked to Yossi later as they filed back into the room.

"What do you know about handball," replied Yossi contemptuously, and turned away.

The newcomer took his seat but kept yawning and fidgeting to indicate that he had no interest in what was going on in class. The boys all felt that a boy like Roy wouldn't last long in their school. For B.A.T.T. was a place where the students did enjoy their classes, and it was a point of honor never to refuse to take up a challenge for a game of handball even if he was sure to get a thorough licking.

"He's just yellow," was the opinion of most of the kids, except Benny who said, "He just doesn't care, and doesn't want anyone else to care about him."

The next day, one of the younger kids came to school all excited. "I saw the new boy ride in a slick new Oldsmobile. They stopped in front of the new expensive apartment house near the Project. When I checked the names, I found a mailbox with a brand new sign 'Dorf'."

Well, perhaps to some of you a new Oldsmobile is nothing special. But to the kids of the Project anything more expensive than a Ford was "classy." It immediately put Roy Dorf in a class by himself, at least as far as the younger kids were concerned. The older ones did not make a fuss about their new classmate when Roy came in late the next day, without even an excuse. Rabbi Greenberg continued his lesson and everyone ignored the new student who kept cracking a big hunk of bubble gum throughout the lesson.

"Challenge," said Roy to Yossi during recess. A hushed silence fell over the noisy crowd of boys milling around the Talmud Torah. They gathered in a large semi-circle around the handball court and followed every move of the two boys. Yossi was the undisputed champion of B.A.T.T., but there was no doubt now that he had at least found his match. Roy was taller and heavier and possessed skill and power that made up for the greater agility of Yossi. It hadn't happened for a long time that the boys missed the ringing of the bell which signalled the end of recess. They didn't even notice Rabbi Greenberg standing behind them, following the match as eagerly as the boys themselves.

"Congratulations," said Rabbi Greenberg to Roy Dorf when the new boy walked past him, back into the building, after a few wicked angle punches won him the game.

"Best of three games," Yossi had suggested to the new champ when they shook hands. Roy accepted.

Still, Roy Dorf kept on showing his annoyance with the Hebrew school. He acted as if he hated every moment of it and had all intentions of keeping his promise and winning the bet between himself and Rabbi Greenberg. His knowledge of Hebrew was far less than that of his classmates but he made no effort to pay attention and catch up.

Only once did he forget his usual tactic of non-cooperation. It was during a Jewish history class. Rabbi Greenberg was discussing Rabbi Jochanan ben Zakkai and his decision to flee the besieged Jerusalem while the Jewish capital fought its death battle, and ask Vespasian, the Roman Emperor, for the city Yavneh as a new center of Torah study. No one in the class had ever dared to oppose the teacher so violently as Roy Dorf, who quite skillfully and convincingly argued the case of the extremists of those days who would rather die fighting than make a compromise with the Romans, even for the sake of the survival of the Jewish people and its soul, the study of Torah. Obviously Roy was not the dumb-bell which he pretended to be. His vocabulary and arguments showed that he had a keen mind and good education. But he lacked understanding and appreciation for the view that Torah-study and its survival is more important than physical victory or defeat in one battle or war of arms.

The discussion went on even after class, and it took Benny's sharp logic to convince the boys who had gathered around that the Jewish view was not one that seeks the glory of battle at any price. Benny, Yossi and Roy continued the argument for a long time until it got dark and they walked home together.

"Are these your friends?" asked a pleasant voice from behind.

The boys turned around and saw a neat, well-dressed, young woman come up and put her arm around Roy.

"We are in the same class and we had a discussion," answered Roy, rather embarrassed.

"Why don't you boys come up to the house. I'd like to meet Roy's friends," said the friendly young woman. But it was too late that day. The boys had to rush home.

"Make sure to come up some other time, perhaps on Saturday or Sunday," she invited. "You can watch television together or have some other fun."

Benny and Yossi were too shy to say outright that they could not come up to watch television on Shabbos. But they realized why Roy was so reluctant to become closer friends with the boys of the Talmud Torah.

One day Roy did not come to the Talmud Torah. One day passed, then another, and another, and a full week, and he still did not come to class. There was no answer when Rabbi Greenberg called his home. Yossi and Benny decided to go to his house and try to find out why their classmate had been absent for such a long time. Had he persuaded his father to let him quit, or was there another cause?

They rang the bell to the Dorf apartment, but there was no answer. Next evening they went again after class, and again there was no answer. When there was no answer on the third day, Benny rang the bell of the apartment next door. A woman looked through the peephole and refused to open the door or even to speak to the two boys. Benny pleaded with her to tell them what had happened to the Dorfs.

"Don't you boys read the newspapers!" was all she would say and went away from the door quickly.

The boys looked at each other in bewilderment. Only then did it dawn upon them that they had read that a family from Brooklyn had been severely injured in an automobile accident.

Quickly the boys ran out to the candy store around the corner. The storekeeper confirmed the story that all three, father, mother, and Roy had been hurt in a collision of their car with a truck that had suddenly stopped in front of them while they were travelling at full speed on the highway. They were in a hospital in a small town, fifty miles away, critically ill, in casts, unable to talk.

Every day the boys of B.A.T.T. recited Tehillim for Roy and his parents. When they heard that their condition improved they wrote letters to Roy. A small group of boys went to the hospital to visit Roy and decided to make regular visits to the hospital. At first Roy hardly reacted to his visitors. His leg and right side were in a heavy cast and his mind seemed unable to grasp anything. But gradually he began to take an interest in what was going on around him. He appreciated the little gifts of the boys from the Talmud Torah. He thanked them for the letters they had sent him and asked about what was happening in the school.

One day Rabbi Greenberg came to visit. He brought Roy a few books — a Chumash with translation, a Siddur, and a Jewish History book. As he left he said, "When you feel like studying them, you'll appreciate what they have to offer you. I'll be glad to answer any questions you may have."

At first, Rabbi Greenberg's package lay untouched by his bedside. But as the time dragged on, day after day, Roy began to glance at the books. He was comforted by the inspiring words of Tehillim and fascinated by the explanations of the Chumash. He became sincerely interested and wrote to Rabbi Greenberg asking many questions which showed that he had really begun to study seriously.

It took almost three months until Roy Dorf and his parents were able to leave the hospital and go home.

And then he had to spend a few more weeks in bed. Yossi and Benny took turns visiting Roy and teaching him the many things which he did not know and which had begun to make a great deal of sense to him now that he had become interested on his own and was not forced by his father to study them. Even his mother who had learned little of the Jewish religion and history listened intently to the conversations of her son and his friends and frequently interrupted with questions of her own.

Finally, Roy was able to get off his bed and walk around. The cast was removed and gradually he regained his strength. Never in his talks with the boys did he mention that he would go back to the Talmud Torah. His father left it completely up to him. But from his questions it appeared to Benny that he was toying with the idea. Once when Roy was out of the room, Benny asked Mrs. Dorf whether she thought that Roy would come back to B.A.T.T., and to let him know if he would.

One day Roy decided that he would like to visit the "old place" where he had met Benny, Yossi, Rabbi Greenberg, and all the other nice fellows who had shown so much interest and concern for him while he had been incapacitated, "just for a social visit" he explained to his parents.

Mrs. Dorf happily informed Benny of her son's plans. Roy's mother drove him to the Talmud Torah. As he walked up to the entrance everything seemed just the same as on the last day he had been there. But when he opened the door, something was different. The hall was empty. He walked straight through to the classroom. There, instead of benches, were long tables, covered with white tablecloths, loaded with all kinds of delicacies, and around the table stood the kids from the Talmud Torah. Large signs of welcome met his eye. At a signal the boys began to sing.

"Whose party is this?" asked Roy in surprise when Rabbi Greenberg greeted him.

"It's yours. The boys are happy that you are well and back with them," explained Rabbi Greenberg.

Roy could not answer immediately. Tears filled his eyes. The boys crowded around him, dancing with him around the room. When they all quieted down, Benny greeted Roy officially in the name of B.A.T.T.

"We want a speech," chanted the boys.

Roy got up slowly and said simply and quietly. "I think Rabbi Greenberg won the bet. I thought I came back just for a visit. Now I realize that I came back because deep down I knew that I belong here with you. I have so much to learn. I want to be one of you, one of the Bnei Abraham Talmud Torah boys."

In time, Roy became not only the undisputed handball champ but one of the best and most intelligent students of the Talmud Torah.

Yoine Schifflbaum

One day, as the boys from Bnei Abraham Talmud Torah walked along the street, they saw an unusual sight. In some of the old streets in the neighborhood there are boarded-up houses and empty stores galore. Many of the old tenements had been torn down, especially around the area where B.A.T.T. is located, and huge projects with wide avenues were built in place of the dirty slums.

There was one little house on the other side of the Avenue, only a few minutes walk from B.A.T.T., which had been boarded up for a long time. That day, as the boys walked to the Talmud Torah, they saw workers removing the boards and fixing the old house. Standing with them and lending a hand, was a man with a long black beard and "Peyes" (sidelocks). The boys of B.A.T.T. were used to seeing Rabbis with beard and Peyes. But this man was not a Rabbi. He was dressed in regular work clothes and apparently knew how to handle tools very well. Naturally the boys were very curious. So, Benny, who spoke Yiddish fluently, walked over to the bearded man in overalls and greeted him with a friendly "Sholom Aleichem."

The man was pleased to meet such friendly Jewish boys and a lively conversation developed between him and Benny.

What they found out was very interesting. The stranger had bought the little house and intended to open a carpentry shop on the ground floor.

"My name is Yoine Schifflbaum, and I hope you boys will be my friends and help me get business around here," he said.

Now there is nothing unusual about a carpenter's shop in that neighborhood. There are all kinds of shops and craftsmen there. But this was the first time the boys saw a carpenter with a beard and Peyes, and to them it was a big thing; especially since he had asked them for their friendship and help. The boys were eager to assist him since he was a new immigrant to the United States, and he was trying to make an honest living with the trade he knew. They were anxious to help him to succeed.

When the house was fixed up and the sign went up: YOINE SCHIFFLBAUM, *All Types of Carpentry and Furniture Repair Work,* the boys looked for jobs for him. Practically each one of them found something needing to be repaired in their houses. And the rumor was that little Shloimele, finding nothing broken, worked so long on the old rocking-chair in which his uncle rested after he came home from work, that the side arm came off. His hand was scratched and bleeding, but under no circumstances would he reveal what caused it. Shloimele was so happy when, with the help of Yossi, he dragged the rocking chair down the stairs and up the block to the repair shop of Yoine Schifflbaum.

After a while, as the boys passed the carpentry shop on their way to the Talmud Torah in the afternoons, they saw Yoine Schifflbaum's face turn sadder from day to day. The little jobs which the boys had brought in were soon completed. And even though the boys did their best to drum up new business for him, advertising to all that he was a very capable carpenter who did excellent work for a very reasonable price, there did not seem to be enough work for him to earn a living.

"I don't understand it," said Benny to his father at the supper table. "There is a drunken old carpenter a few blocks further down. He seems to be always busy. I wonder why Yoine can't get enough work. Our boys all like him very much. He has a cheery word for everyone, and there does not seem to be a thing he does not know about Torah. Whatever we ask him, he knows, and he explains to us so well that all the difficulty seems to disappear like magic. He would be such a good teacher. But when Rabbi Greenberg asked whether he would like to teach, Yoine replied that he preferred to work with his hands, and to spend his spare time studying Torah for himself. Oh, Dad, perhaps you have some idea what we can do to help him?"

Benny's father, who had a small textile business, thought for a while. He liked the idea that his son and his friends took such a keen interest in the welfare of the new immigrant. On the other hand, what was there the boys could do to help the carpenter if the neighborhood could not provide enough jobs for him. Or maybe they did not trust him as yet? After all, a newly arrived immigrant who did not speak the language would not attract much business from the Italians and Irish who made up the bulk of the people in the neighborhood. He explained this to Benny.

"Oh, Dad, you have a reputation as a good businessman. Surely you must have some better ideas than excuses for the neighborhood."

"Well, son," replied his father with a shrug. "If I were Yoine, I would go to some factories to get orders for new furniture. People don't have much repair work done these days."

Benny brought this suggestion to the boys' council meeting after Talmud Torah classes that day. Yossi had also discussed the problem of Yoine with his parents. His mother had suggested that there were plenty of dirty and broken down fences, doors, and wooden shutters in the neighborhood. If they could convince the people to start a beautification project there would be plenty of work for Yoine. Many other ideas were suggested. But these two seemed best to the youngsters of B.A.T.T. They talked it over with their Rebbe, Rabbi Greenberg. He was always happy if his students not only learned about Mitzvot, but actually practiced what they learned. But neither he nor any of the boys knew of any furniture factory or other place which would need carpentry work. However, the idea of a neighborhood improvement project sounded more promising.

The next day, a committee of the boys went to Boro Hall and asked to see the Boro President. They had been told that they would need his permission to start a real project with posters all over advertising meetings and rallies. When they had started putting up some posters, a policeman took them down and warned them not to start anything without the official O.K. So, a committee of the boys waited patiently in the waiting-room of the Boro President's office. There were many other people waiting to see the City official, and they were surprised to see a group of young boys, sitting quietly among them, occasionally whispering seriously to each other. There were also a few press photographers waiting around to see if anything newsworthy would happen. But everything seemed just dull routine, and certainly not worth exploding their flashbulbs for.

Suddenly there was a commotion. The door that led from the waiting-room to the inner offices was pushed open, and out stormed a heavy-jowled, red-faced man, followed by the Boro President.

"Who are the boys that have come to see me about their neighborhood project?" he asked. The four boys of the committee from B.A.T.T. jumped up.

"Well, Garner, here is your chance to make up for the terrible way you treated your tenants. I want you to become the sponsor of the project which these boys propose, regardless of the cost, you understand!"

The boys hardly knew who Garner was, or what was going on. All they had done was to give the Boro President's secretary the basic facts about the reason for their request for an appointment. And here, before they had even seen him, was the answer to their problem.

The heavy, red-faced man was made to pose with them and the smiling Boro President. From all sides came the cross-fire of the photographers' flashbulbs. The next day, all the New York papers and television newscasts carried the picture of the four boys from B.A.T.T. with the Boro President and the rich real estate owner who was to finance their neighborhood project. Reporters found out the real reason behind the program idea. It was a human interest story and Yoine Schifflbaum became a celebrity overnight.

The boys of B.A.T.T. accomplished their goal far beyond their dreams. Furniture manufacturers were proud to give the bearded Jewish carpenter sub-contracts, and they were extremely satisfied with his work. Soon Yoine had to hire helpers to meet his obligations, and rent larger shop facilities in the adjoining factory building.

"You see," said Rabbi Greenberg, when he discussed the unexpected results of their campaign to help Yoine, " 'Mitzvah goreres Mitzvah,' (One Mitzvoh leads to another)." For, in gratitude Yonie Schifflbaum gave ten per cent of his earnings to the Talmud Torah and spent an hour a day learning Gemoro with the oldest boys, free of charge.

Dishes for Passover

"Pitcher got a belly-ache! Pitcher got a belly-ache!" The boys of Class Bais had quite a time harrassing Yossi, the best baseball player of the Bnei Abraham Talmud Torah. This catcall usually was reserved for the lesser stars of B.A.T.T., but never for Yossi who was always the hero of the playground with his curves, knuckleballs and sizzling fastballs.

But there was no mistaking it. Something was wrong with Yossi's pitches all week long. For the first time in the many months of fierce competition between Gimmel and Daled, Gimmel won more than a single game. And it was definitely due to the fact that Yossi's curves fell short or wide, and his fastballs missed the strike-zone. Disgusted with himself, Yossi threw the glove down and walked off the playground long before his usual time.

"What's the matter, Yossi?" asked Benny, the star pupil of B.A.T.T., when he caught up with his friend.

"Nothing," retorted Yossi sharply. "Everyone is entitled to a slump once in a while. I ain't Superman, right!" Yossi turned his back on his friend and walked away, making it obvious that he did not care to share the cause of his misery with anybody, not even with his closest friend.

This was the third time that Yossi had reacted so rudely to Benny's attempts to talk things over, and Benny was quite perplexed. Slowly Benny walked back to the Talmud Torah and went into Rabbi Greenberg's office.

"Rebbe, may I speak to you for a moment?" he asked.

"Sure, come right in," answered Rabbi Greenberg, who was always available for his boys.

"Rebbe, I want to talk to you about Yossi. Something is definitely wrong. He does not act like his usual self. He walks around all by himself. He even walked out in the middle of the game just now. He looks so unhappy that I can't take it any longer. I tried to talk to him about it but he refuses to confide his troubles in me. Maybe you know what is bothering him or you can advise me how we can help him."

Rabbi Greenberg looked at his Talmid and a feeling of pride and affection for the youngster who was so worried about his friend made him forget the problem for a moment. He stepped out from behind his desk, placed his arm around the boy's shoulder and said:

"It is good of you to be so concerned about your friend's welfare. That is real 'Ahavas Yisroel'."

But Benny was too worried to feel proud. At this moment he wanted advice more than praise.

"But what can be done, Rebbe?" he asked.

"Well, I've noticed too that Yossi is disturbed by something. I wish I could help him, or tell you how to help him. I just think that it is not right for us to butt in on Yossi's business, as long as he refuses to share it with us. Somehow I have a feeling that sooner or later you will find the oppor-

tunity to make him talk. Apparently it is something embarrass-
ing, or else he would have come to me or to you. So, be
patient until Yossi draws you into his confidence. We might
hurt him otherwise," Rabbi Greenberg advised.

Benny was not very happy with this advice but he realized
that Rabbi Greenberg was right, that it was not wise for him to
mix into his friend's business as long as Yossi plainly showed
that he did not want him to.

That evening, after he had finished his homework, Benny
took a walk over to the other end of the Project where Yossi
lived. He had the feeling that his best friend needed him, and
he wanted to be around if Yossi wanted him. He sat down on
the last bench of the large playground behind the row of
modern buildings and waited, humming and whittling away
on a piece of wood he had picked up from the ground. He
did not have to wait long. A few minutes later, Yossi strolled
along, sat down on the bench, saying no more than the usual
"Hi," but without his customary zip.

"Let's take a walk," suggested Benny after a while. Reluct-
antly, Yossi got up and the two boys left the Project grounds.
Benny did not say a single word, remembering what Rabbi
Greenberg had advised him. After a while, when they were
far enough from the Project, Yossi stopped short and said,
"I'm sorry Benny. I acted like a heel. But I just can't help it.
If you only knew."

"It's okay, Yoss. You don't have to tell me if you don't
want to. I just thought perhaps I might help you, or it might
be easier for you if you could confide your troubles to a friend,"
said Benny.

Yossi walked on without answering, Benny plodding

along at his side. Then suddenly Yossi blurted out, "How can I tell you. I know you are going to look down on me if I do. Anyway, I am the dumbest in the class."

"Don't be foolish, Yoss. You just started late, but you'll catch up with the rest," Benny assured him.

"Remember, Benny, what we learnt last week about preparing the house for Pesach. Rabbi Greenberg told us about the special set of dishes that are not used all year round. I went home to my mother and told her that she would have to get two new sets of dishes and pots, one for meat and one for dairy.

" 'You are crazy, boy,' she screamed at me. 'You know your father makes little enough as a driver for the candy company. And it is only a few months ago that you made us buy new dishes and throw out the old ones. I think we'll have to stop sending you to that Hebrew school. Every time you come home with new ideas. Tell your teacher that this is America, and that he should not teach you all that old-fashioned stuff that was good for the Old Country. First you make me light candles on Friday night. Then you ask your Dad to stop working on Shabbos. Now you want us to buy two more sets of dishes. Enough of that nonsense.'

"I tried to reason with her and I kept explaining it to her, but she just refuses to listen. As a matter of fact, she said that if I bother her any more about the dishes she'll definitely take me out of the Talmud Torah. That's it. Now you know it all and you can despise me if you want. I can't help it that my parents are not religious like yours," concluded Yossi sadly.

Benny did not answer. Silently the two boys walked through the dusk and a feeling of strong sympathy and concern seized Benny for his friend. "It's tough, I can see that," he exclaimed.

And again they walked on for a while, silently. Yossi felt much better now that someone knew his troubles. By sharing it with his best friend, he gained confidence and comfort.

"Let's go back, Yossi," said Benny after a while, putting his arm around his friend's shoulders. He did not have to express what he felt. But Yossi knew that Benny really wanted to say that he did not look down upon him, that he was sorry for him, and that he would try to help him, if there was any way he could.

Next afternoon, before classes began, Benny went to Rabbi Greenberg and told him about his conversation with Yossi and about the trouble that distressed his friend so much.

"What can we do to help Yossi? We must do something," pleaded Benny.

"Perhaps I should go over and talk to Yossi's parents," suggested Rabbi Greenberg.

But Benny was afraid that Yossi's mother would be even more annoyed and might very likely take Yossi out of the Talmud Torah altogether.

"If only we had the money, we could buy the dishes," lamented Benny.

"Wait a minute," said Rabbi Greenberg. "That's an excellent idea. Let's help them financially."

Rabbi Greenberg and Benny were exploring various ways to raise funds for the dishes which Yossi's parents could not and would not buy for Passover.

"But what is Yossi going to say if we are going to collect money for him. He will be very embarrassed," thought Benny aloud.

"Well, Yossi doesn't have to know for whom we are raising the money. Just the two of us know for whom it is. Every one else will only know of a Seder Campaign, a project of the Bnei Abraham Talmud Torah students for an emergency purpose. As you know, it is a mitzvah to give tzedokoh for 'Maos Chitin,' for needy people to buy all the necessary items for Pesach."

A quick trip to the nearest hardware store showed the Rabbi and his best pupil that they would have to raise a minimum of a hundred dollars to set up the kitchen of Yossi's family with dairy and meat dishes for Passover.

That very afternoon, after the classes were over, Benny spread the word that all the students were to meet on the playground behind the Talmud Torah for a special meeting. Not a single B.A.T.T. boy was missing, even though some grumbled that they had homework to do. The grumbling subsided as soon as the boys became aware of the purpose of the meeting. Rabbi Greenberg was invited to come to the meeting to address the students on the urgent project.

He explained, "There is a special mitzvah before Pesach to contribute money for 'Maos Chitin' — that is to give to people who haven't enough money to buy matzos for Pesach. And the highest form of this mitzvah is to give it in secret — so the person never knows from whom it came and the donor, to whom it goes. There are many people in the Project who need help before Pesach and it would be fitting for B.A.T.T. students to participate in such a Seder campaign. Therefore I have asked Benny to make this your special Pesach project, and I assure you, you could not lend a helping hand to a worthier cause. How and what to do I leave up to you. I am certain that if you sincerely wish to help, you will be able to think of a way to raise a tidy sum."

"Let's vote," proposed Benny.

As expected, the Seder Campaign was adopted unanimously by the B.A.T.T. boys and immediately they set about finding ways to raise funds. As usual, it was Yossi, not suspecting at all that it is for him and his parents that the money was being collected, who came up with the soundest plan and he was immediately elected manager of the project. Seder Campaign he suggested, was to run a huge open Flea Market on their playground with a performance of a play as well as games, that would attract the people of the Project. All the children would search their cellars and attics and drawers for old things, or canvas the neighborhood homes and stores for contributions to the Flea Market.

"We can fix broken things, repaint old, worn toys, have our sisters press or wash unused clothing," suggested one boy.

"My mother will bake a cake that we can raffle off," called out another.

"Mine, too," said a third.

"My brother knows how to print very well. He'll make signs for people in five minutes, while they wait," volunteered another.

"I can draw faces," exclaimed Yankie. "For a quarter I'll draw anyone's portrait."

Benny suggested that they should provide the whole Project with "Charoses" for the Seder. "I'll ask my mother and

Mrs. Greenberg to teach me how to make it. We'll go from house to house and offer to deliver the 'Charoses' on Erev Pesach, so the women won't have to bother making it themselves. We can sell a portion of 'Charoses' for a quarter; I am sure that can bring us in quite some nice profit."

His total involvement in this charitable undertaking made Yossi forget all his own worries. He accepted or rejected the suggestions of the B.A.T.T. students, and appointed committees to take care of the various projects. There were only four weeks left to work. There was not a single baseball game played on the B.A.T.T. playground during these days. The boys had more important things on their minds. They had quick planning meetings right after classes were over and then went to work. They were all surprised to see what useful things were to be found in attics, backyards, cellars, vacant lots and all kinds of odd places. Whatever could not be used for the Flea Market was sold to a neighborhood junk dealer who realized that the boys of the Talmud Torah were involved in a worthy cause, and he gladly paid a bit more for things which he might otherwise have considered unsalable.

The fever of the Seder project seized not only the boys, but all those who were associated with them: their families, friends and acquaintances. Every day brought new ideas. Sunday afternoon, two weeks before Pesach, was the day of the Flea Market, and there was not a youngster in the whole Project, Jewish or not, who was not lured to the Playground behind the Talmud Torah to try his luck at the many games, lotteries, and fortune wheels which the boys of B.A.T.T. had rigged up. The grownups were attracted by the great bargains announced in the bulletins posted in every hallway.

At nightfall the Flea Market was closed. All the boys of

B.A.T.T. gathered in the largest classroom of the school. Yossi, the campaign manager, and Benny, counted the profits.

"One hundred and ninety-two dollars and fifty cents," shouted Yossi when the count was concluded.

"Wait," shouted Benny excitedly, "we forgot something. We haven't made and sold the 'Charoses' yet. I myself have twelve orders. Yankie and David are in charge, don't forget."

The Sunday before Passover, they gathered in the kitchen of the B.A.T.T. Shul and made the "Charoses" under the supervision of Rabbi Greenberg's wife who had a special recipe. She claimed that her great-grandmother had invented it in Poland, and it was known all over as Sarah Shaindel's Charoses for its delicious, tart flavor. It was so good, in fact, that some people in the Project gave half a dollar for a regular portion, instead of a quarter, because it smelled so delicious.

Two days before Pesach, a truck rolled up before the house in which Yossi lived. It just so happened that Benny was visiting Yossi and Yossi's parents were not at home. The bell rang.

"Who could that be?" asked Yossi.

"Why don't you push the button and see," replied Benny.

Two husky truck drivers carried a large, heavy box up the stairs.

"The Newmans live here?" asked the first.

"Yes," replied Yossi, for Newman was his name. "What's this? Are you sure you are at the right address? As far as I know, my parents haven't ordered anything. They couldn't pay for it even if they would have."

"It's all paid for, young fellow. This is the right address, and Newman is your name. So the two boxes, this and another one just like it, from Chaim's House Furnishing Store must be yours," the truck driver informed him.

The two men set the large boxes down and left. Then Benny explained. At first Yossi turned red and wanted to send it all back.

"Your mother will not object anymore to your going to Talmud Torah if she sees that she got the dishes free. Just tell her someone delivered it. So she can't send it back," advised Benny.

It was a happy Pesach for the B.A.T.T. students, especially for Yossi, Benny and Rabbi Greenberg. Yankie and David were especially proud when they reported that they had raised another $26 from the sale of the "Charoses". Rabbi Greenberg distributed the extra money to other needy families in the Project. They were thankful that they could now buy the necessities for the Seder although they were unaware from where the money came. The other boys enjoyed the Seder much more than usual knowing that they had helped some unknown families celebrate Passover properly.

The Lag B'omer Outing

One of the events most looked forward to by the students of the Bnei Abraham Talmud Torah was the annual Lag B'Omer outing. Planning started on the day after Pesach, and the excitement built up with each succeeding day until the dawn of Lag B'Omer. On that day, the boys met at the Talmud Torah, equipped with knapsacks, baseball bats and gloves, and plenty of food. Everybody knew from past experience that somehow, something special, something unexpected, always occurred that made each outing an unforgettable occasion.

This year, too, the boys had an exciting day planned. They made a special Minyan at five in the morning. And by six-thirty they were boarding the large yellow bus that was to take them to Bear Mountains. They were to return in the evening by boat down the Hudson River. Everyone was in high spirits and bursting with excitement. This year's trip was the farthest they had ever planned to take, and there was so much to be seen as they travelled across the Williamsburg Bridge, up the Westside Highway, along the Hudson River, across the George Washington Bridge and then on Route 9W all the way up into the mountains. It was a beautiful spring day, and they enjoyed every bit of the trip.

As scheduled, they arrived at Bear Mountain State Park

at about ten o'clock. All morning they played baseball, handball or volleyball on the well-kept grounds. Then came lunch time. There was a beautifully arranged picnic ground near a stream, where the boys could wash their hands before eating, and sit down at tables to eat in comfort. There they also listened to a talk given by Rabbi Greenberg about Lag B'Omer and took part in a quiz.

After Bentching and a short rest, they were ready to set out on the best part of their program, a "fox hunt" through the forest. The hunters would be Romans, and the hunted would be Rabbi Shimon bar Yochai and his son Elazar, the heroes of Lag B'Omer, who hid from the Romans in a cave for thirteen years and studied Torah. The "foxes" were to leave traces behind them in the form of markings in colored chalk on trees or stones. The other boys were to be the "hunters" who would follow the trail of colored markings until they would reach the "cave," some fine spot in the forest which would be the end of the hunt.

Yossi and Benny were chosen to be Rabbi Shimon and Rabbi Elazer, and Yankie was to be in charge of the hunters and direct the hunt. Yossi and Benny were given a start of half an hour, and then the "hunt" began.

At first, it was not difficult to follow the trail, but then the going became rough. For about two hours, the manhunt went on in the forest. The "Romans" were thoroughly worn out. Yet, there was no sign of the "cave." The markings led them to the end of the forest, where huge meadows and freshly ploughed fields greeted the weary hunters. Search as they might, they could find no further markings, and there was no sign of Yossi and Benny. They had disappeared as if into thin air.

"I told you," growled Yankie, "we should not have let those two sly 'foxes' go together. What's the fun!"

They turned to trace the trail back to the spot where Benny must have misled them intentionally. But it was all in vain. When they were half way through the forest back toward the beginning of their hunt, Yankie blew his whistle, which was the signal for all to gather at his side. They were all a bit puzzled and worried. It was not at all like Yossi and Benny to let them down, mislead them, or play unfair.

One boy remarked, "We passed a lake at the edge of the forest. Maybe they went swimming, or boating."

Shloimele asked, "Are there any bears in Bear Mountain forest? I think we should go back and call Rabbi Greenberg."

Shloimele's question sent shivers down their spines! And they all agreed that they should go back. Yankie suggested that only three boys go back to the playground to get Rabbi Greenberg, while the rest divide up into two groups to search the forest and the area surrounding the lake. They were to meet in a half hour to make sure that they would not lose track of each other. David, the champion whistler, would stay at Yankie's side and keep whistling the B.A.T.T. signal.

Yankie and his group went back to the edge of the forest where they had lost the original trail. Perhaps they had missed some markings. Indeed, after carefully pushing apart the thick young grass at the border between the forest and the fields, Yankie found a stone with red markings pointing to one side. Carefully, he and his boys walked along the edge of the forest in the direction of the marker. A few minutes later, they found another marker to show them that they were on the right track. At once, David whistled the signal to call the others to return to their meeting spot. Two of the boys remained at the place where they found the marker, and the rest went back to fetch the other searching party and to wait for Rabbi Greenberg who should arrive at the appointed spot in the center of the forest shortly.

"I really don't understand those two boys. They are always so reliable. I have a feeling something unexpected must have happened. Let's hurry to the markings you just discovered," said Rabbi Greenberg anxiously.

The second marker pointed further into the same direction as the first. The entire group, led by Rabbi Greenberg and Yankie, moved along cautiously, looking for new clues. As far as they could see there were only fields, meadows and the forest on the other side. Search as they might, there just was no further indication where the trail had taken the boys who were the "foxes."

Suddenly Shloimele called excitedly, "Look, look there! Benny is coming!"

A truck was approaching on the small path that led through the fields, and on top sat Benny waving to the boys. Rabbi Greenberg heaved a sigh of relief when he saw his best student alive and well. But he was still worried about Yossi. He and the boys held their breath until the truck stopped in front of them and Benny jumped off.

The farmer sitting behind the wheel greeted them with a smile and a loud, "Sholom Aleichem. Come on, hop into the truck and I'll take you to our farm where your friend Yossi is waiting!"

They climbed on to the truck, and Benny began his story.

The more the boys listened, the wider their eyes opened in amazement.

"You see, Yossi and I were kind of tired when we came to the edge of the forest. After a short rest, we wanted to search for a good spot to call the 'cave' and end the trail. But as we were sitting on the grass, looking out over the freshly plowed fields, we heard someone calling for help. Yossi and I raced across the fields in the direction from where the voice had come.

"We found a tractor, under which an elderly farmer lay pinned to the ground. Luckily, Yossi knows how to handle his father's delivery truck, and he was able to follow the farmer's instructions and move the tractor slowly off his foot, while I supported him. Then we carefully lifted the farmer up into the seat of the tractor. Yossi drove the tractor very, very, slowly back to the farm, which is quite a distance from here. In our concern for the farmer, we forgot to leave a clue for you, as the farmer was moaning with pain. He was trying to adjust something on the motor when the tractor moved and the wheel pinned his foot down right above the ankle. All we could think about was getting him quickly back to his farm where he could get a doctor's help."

At this point, the young farmer interrupted Benny's tale, and said, "The two boys were wonderful! Such courage and presence of mind is rare even among grown ups. They saved my father's foot, and perhaps his life, for we were able to get immediate medical attention for him and he is going to be alright. But let us go up to the farm, so that we may have the rare privilege and pleasure to be hosts to so fine a crowd."

On the way to the farm the farmer told the Rabbi and the boys that he and his family were refugees from Europe, and only two years in the country. They were the only Jewish farmers in this area, and, although financially they were doing nicely and making a comfortable living, they were lonesome for Jewish company.

"We were drifting away," the farmer continued sadly, "away from Jewish life, and our children are growing up, you know. But now, with what has happened, and these bright lads, we suddenly began to feel as if we were living in a dream and have wakened from a heavy sleep. We feel again that we are Jews and living among Jews, and you must help us keep up this feeling . . ."

"Yes, it was quite a surprise," Benny said. "As we were hoisting the old man into the seat of the tractor he moaned, 'Oy vai iz mir.' (Woe to me.) So I started talking Yiddish to the old man who was so happy because it was so much easier for him to understand than English. If he had not been in pain he would have embraced and kissed us, I bet. By the time we arrived at the farm we had heard all about their flight from Poland and their settling on the farm, after several years of wandering from one country to another."

"And then," the younger farmer broke in, "the boys came to the farm, and within a few minutes we were all friends, and my children were happy as they had not been for a long time. But then Benny reminded himself that you would not know where he and Yossi had disappeared to. That is why I came here with the truck to bring you to the farm."

The truck was now turning into a side road and up a steep hill, and soon pulled up near a large house.

"This is where we live. Please come in and make yourselves at home," the farmer said heartily.

A warm welcome awaited them inside the house, and Yossi was there, of course, and beaming with joy.

"Come," he said to the boys, with an air as if he owned the farm. "I'll show you around," for he had already become familiar with the cows and chickens and everything else.

The boys inspected the farm with all its interesting things, such as city children rarely see. The chicken coops, the milking machines, the creaming and butter machines, the egg-grading machines. They stroked the cows and calves, and horses and ponies. Then they again gathered in the large living room, where pots of steaming hot chocolate awaited them. Rabbi Greenberg spoke about the significance of Lag B'Omer, and asked Benny to tell the story of Rabbi Akiva and his disciples and the life of Rabbi Shimon bar Yochai whose "Yahrzeit" we observe on this day.

The farmer and his family were deeply moved when they heard Benny speak so enthusiastically about the Jewish past and its lessons, and quote the words of our Sages so knowledgeably. The farmer's children were so impressed that they, too, expressed a strong desire to study in a Talmud Torah just like their visitors.

When the clock indicated that it was time to leave if they wanted to catch the six o'clock boat on the other side of the forest, the old farmer and his family implored Rabbi Greenberg to allow the boys to please stay on a little while longer. The young farmer promised to drive them to the next train station where they could catch a train an hour later and be back in New York at the same time, if not earlier, than if they went by boat.

"The choice is yours, boys," said Rabbi Greenberg. "I promised to take you back by boat. But if you want to remain here and be the guests of our new friends for a little longer, it's fine with me."

They all preferred to stay on, for they all felt how much their staying another while meant to these lonely farmers who were hungry for Jewish people and words of Torah.

At the old farmer's request, the boys took down the Mezuzos and Rabbi Greenberg inspected them and also the farmer's Tefillin. The boys taught the children a few blessings and some songs. They all had a great time.

It was almost time to go. Each of the boys quickly drank a glass of milk fresh from the cow, and went out to watch and help gather the eggs. The children made them promise to come up more often. "You are welcome to be our guests, any time, and for as long as you want. The longer the better," said the old farmer.

As the truck pulled out, the children sadly waved goodbye. "We'll be back," the boys promised, "and we'll write to you."

Rabbi Greenberg promised to send Hebrew books for the children and also for the old man who once knew how to learn, but being without Seforim and companions had forgotten much.

The boys were very tired when they came home that Lag B'Omer night. But they all agreed that it was a most exciting outing. This was only the first of many trips back to the farm in Bear Mountains.

The Cellar Rats

Right after school closed, Bnei Abraham Talmud Torah Day Camp began. The boys of B.A.T.T. considered life in the Talmud Torah Day Camp lots of fun. They enjoyed each other's company and their Rebbe, Rabbi Greenberg, saw to it that they did not get bored, and had a swell time during their long summer vacation despite the heat and dust of the crowded Brooklyn streets.

Except for a few boys who went to sleep-away camp in the Catskill Mountains, there was not a single boy who was not there, eagerly looking forward to lots of fun and excitement. Yossi, Yankie, Benny and the others had great ideas for bunk competition, sports championships and Torah contests. But none could have anticipated what was in store for them. Rabbi Greenberg greeted them enthusiastically, and showed them the new green sweatshirts that had their insignia, the Luchos (Tablets), and B.A.T.T. written in large letters across them.

BANG! A hail of stones crashed through the windows of the Talmud Torah only a short while after the opening bell sounded. Glass splinters flew all over, but luckily no one was hurt.

"Hey, look here," yelled Yossi. "A message."

"Let's see," shouted the bewildered boys, as Yossi picked up the strip of dirty paper wrapped around one of the stones.

"Put up and fight. It's war between yourselves and us. The Cellar Rats," the note read. When Yossi had finished reading the almost illegible note, a gasp of fear escaped from many a boy's mouth.

"Who are the Cellar Rats?" asked Rabbi Greenberg, who had run out of the building to see who threw the stones, but caught sight only of the backs of several boys disappearing around the corner.

"They are the roughest gang around here," answered Yossi.

"And do you know who their leader is? Remember Melly Schreiber who was a student here a few years ago? His father came one day and beat him up right in front of the whole class. Melly never came back after that," recalled Benny.

"Yes," Rabbi Greenberg said. "I remember him well. I'm sorry until this day that I permitted his father to come into the classroom. Somehow, I have the feeling that this tough boy wasn't really as rough as he acted, and that if given half a chance he might have become a good student and an asset to the Talmud Torah and the community."

A pang of regret and pity overcame him. "So this was what had become of him!" muttered Rabbi Greenberg. "He is the leader of the Cellar Rats, and his gang has declared war on the Talmud Torah, for the kick of it."

"Whatever it means, I don't like it a bit," Rabbi Greenberg said out loud. Though they would not admit it outright, the boys had an equally uneasy feeling. They did not want their summer vacation spoiled by that bunch of neighborhood roughnecks.

"Maybe we should go and speak to them and try to convince them to call it off," some of them suggested.

"Waste of time," said Yossi. "I know some of those boys. They'd only laugh at us, if not worse."

The boys continued their activities as if nothing unusual had happened. But all through the day an uneasy current flowed through the group and it marred the joyous beginning of the Day Camp. They had planned trips, activities, plays, games to make the summer in the city enjoyable and exciting. But they did not care for the kind of excitement the Cellar Rats apparently had in mind for them. Most distressing of all was that the gang consisted almost exclusively of Jewish boys — from Melly, the leader, down to the youngest member — picked up in those overcrowded streets around the Project where the Talmud Torah was located.

"I have an idea," said Benny, when the leader of the Talmud Torah boys got together with their Rebbe before they went home that day. "You Yossi, know where Melly Schreiber lives. Perhaps Rabbi Greenberg should go to see him alone and dissuade him from this stupid business. Let them have wars with other street gangs who are interested in fighting."

Rabbi Greenberg agreed that this was the best suggestion of all the many made so far.

Only Yossi objected. "I don't think you know Melly and what has become of him recently. He isn't the kid he was when he attended here. I doubt whether his father would dare lay a hand on him now."

"But we can try, anyway. It can't make things worse,"

replied Benny. "It's better than having to fight. You can't ask the police to guard us the whole summer. And those toughies will jump on any of our boys when they catch them alone on the way going home."

That very same evening, Yossi led Rabbi Greenberg to the old apartment house where Melly lived.

"He won't even be home now. And if he is, he'll shut the door in our faces," said Yossi.

Nevertheless, Rabbi Greenberg went up the five flights to the end of the narrow hall where the paint peeled off the walls, and the noise and odors of cooking, the yelling and fighting of children, coming out of every door, provided just the right atmosphere. Even Rabbi Greenberg did not feel too comfortable as he rang the doorbell.

Melly himself opened the door. "Whadya want? Get outa here," he snarled when he saw his unexpected visitor; and he made a move to close the door. But something in the face of Rabbi Greenberg must have touched him. Though he disregarded his outstretched hand, he opened the door and asked grouchily, "What do you want here? I don't belong to your joint, nor do I want to have anything to do with you."

"I'd like to talk to you, Melly," said Rabbi Greenberg gently. "It's about that note from your gang."

"I thought so. You may as well forget about it. It was my idea and you won't make me change my mind," retorted Melly. He was about to close the door again when Yossi came upstairs and put his foot in the door.

"Well," he said. "We've come to find out whether you are really as 'yellow' as you act — throwing stones and running away."

"Why don't you accept a challenge by our Day Camp for a summer-long contest between us and you, with points for every activity," added Rabbi Greenberg quickly. "Let's see if you can beat us in a fair contest with impartial judges."

Perhaps Yossi had instinctively hit upon the right approach to the tough boy. Or perhaps Rabbi Greenberg had touched a sensitive chord which Melly always tried to cover up with his roughness. Be that as it may, he was amenable to Rabbi Greenberg's suggestion.

"I have to talk that over with my gang," Melly said after a few seconds of silence.

And so began one of the most exciting summers the boys of the Talmud Torah had ever experienced. It affected not only them and their camp activities, but the entire neighborhood, whose shopkeepers and residents were glad to see the gang of mischief-makers involved in harmless activities.

At first, things were rather tense and difficult. The Cellar Rats had never participated in organized sports or in any form of activity that required fair play or a clean contest. They were used to broken bottle fights, hit and run attacks, and even more dangerous activities. Melly must have had quite a time convincing them to change their habits.

Every day the two groups competed in many different areas. They played baseball, handball, soccer and basketball. They had swimming meets; they wrestled, raced each other. competed in treasure hunts, map reading games, trail hunts and many other activities that made the days of the summer vacation a thrilling adventure.

At the beginning, the Cellar Rats were far ahead in the games of skill, but the boys of B.A.T.T. almost caught up with them when it came to the kind of contests that demanded more intelligence. A neighborhood scoutmaster and Rabbi Greenberg were the judges, and a reporter of a local newspaper reported the running battle between the gang and the boys of the Talmud Torah Day Camp.

Then, one fine morning, when the two teams were to meet for a trip on the ferry to Staten Island where they would continue their competition, the boys of the Cellar Rats did not show up. Somehow the day was spoiled for the others too. They had the uneasy feeling that something had gone wrong. When they returned from Staten Island towards evening, Yossi and Benny decided to visit Melly's home to see what was the matter with the Cellar Rats, who had proved to be not as unpleasant and tough as they had seemed before the summer.

Again the boys climbed up the steps of the old apartment house, with the terrible odors of cooking, washing and open garbage pails. The screaming, yelling, and arguing, the noise from loud radios, phonographs and televisions surrounded them from all sides. They rang the bell. The door opened. But instead of Melly or his husky father or mother, two detectives came out, grabbed Benny and Yossi and pulled them inside. There were more policemen inside.

"Come on, kids, spill the beans," a rough officer demanded. "Where is the stuff? Come on, now, don't play dumb. You won't fool us."

After a few frightening minutes and some real tough attempts by the officers to make the two boys talk, the officers verified the claims of complete innocence by the two Talmud Torah students with a telephone call to Rabbi Greenberg. The police officer explained that they were trying to trap some of the members of the Cellar Rats who were running errands for a gang of older neighborhood delinquents. Melly had been missing the entire previous night and that day.

"They were just using you kids and the contest with you

to cover up for other secret activities," claimed one of the officers.

Yossi and Benny were bitterly disappointed. So that was behind Melly's willingness to play along in the contest instead of the open warfare. And here they had assumed they were really accomplishing something to help the kids keep out of trouble.

The boys noticed Melly's mother sitting in the corner, crying and occasionally moaning, "What have they done to my poor boy! Melly, Melly, had you only listened to me!"

As the hours passed in futile waiting, Yossi and Benny, whose parents had been informed of their whereabouts, could not help but feel worried for Melly. It just did not seem possible that he had fooled them so completely. As the evening dragged on, a police officer suggested that a few of them go out to search for the Cellar Rats. Yossi volunteered to go along. At first the officer refused, but then he had second thoughts.

"It might be a good idea to have you two fellows along, if your parents consent. One can never tell what trouble those kids from the gutter get into. It takes kids to crawl after them into the holes in which they hide."

The two boys cruised all over the slum area in an unmarked police car with the detectives. Their hearts thumped with excitement; they fortified themselves with silent prayers to G-d.

The search ended abruptly outside a large, abandoned factory building at the outskirts of the old Brooklyn neighborhood. Occasional lights flickered across the hollows of the shattered windows and drew the detectives' attention to the building. Sent ahead to scout the situation, Yossi and Benny came just in time to view a scene they were not to forget for a long, long time. It was like a picture they had once seen in a book of medieval history. Several members of the Cellar Rats were chained to the wall, their backs bare and full of swelling red welts. At one end of the long cellar, lit only by a few dusty electric bulbs, in front of a group of young hoodlums lounging about on the ground, bottles in their hands, laughing and cursing loudly, Melly Schreiber was strapped to an iron beam. Two husky hoodlums were standing at his side, slapping his face back and forth, every time the apparent leader of the hoodlums, a slim fellow with two ugly scars across his forehead, gave the signal.

"Will you stop the nonsense and put your rats to work for us, or will you go on playing the baby stuff with those Hebrew school kids?" he snarled.

Obviously hurt, Melly could only shake his head in reply, and the torture went on. How amazed, however, were the two boys looking in from outside, to see the sight of the "Tallis Katan" which covered Melly's upper body. They had not realized that the association with the B.A.T.T. Day Camp had produced such positive results in the tough leader of the Cellar Rats.

Apparently tired of the "game," the scar-faced leader of the gang pulled a long, sharp knife from his belt, placed it against Melly's chest, and repeated his question, "Will you put your rats to work for us, or not?"

By this time, enough policemen had arrived at the scene. Within a few moments, they stormed the building and rounded up every one of the vicious hoodlums. Yossi, afraid that Melly might be hurt by the scar-face, had jumped down from the sill just ahead of the detectives and landed right on top of the scar-face, not caring what would happen to him.

"Yossi," yelled Melly Schreiber, his eyes that had been closed before, now open wide. "Watch out, Yossi!" But the surprise raid was so swift that the hoodlum didn't have a chance to rise from the spot where Yossi had thrown him before the detectives had him handcuffed.

The newspapers reported the story on Page One and the two boys of B.A.T.T. were highly praised for their heroic act. But that did not concern them very much. They were much happier that the Cellar Rats ceased being a gang of toughies. Some, including Melly, joined them for the rest of the summer and promised to continue as students in the Talmud Torah in the fall.

Melly continued to lead those of his friends who stayed with him in the contest which ended in a big baseball game and attracted a large audience who had heard of the wonderful work of the B.A.T.T. boys with the more unfortunate boys of their neighborhood. The boys did not even mind that the former Cellar Rats won this last game, giving them the deciding points to win the contest — because the real victory was theirs. The former Cellar Rats ceased to be a gang. Those who entered the Talmud Torah in the fall, though they had a great deal to learn, caught up nicely and became decent and honest youngsters, instead of continuing to slide down the ugly path on which they had embarked.

Melly Schreiber, whose parents had given him up as unredeemable, became one of the best liked members of B.A.T.T., to Rabbi Greenberg's and Yossi's special joy. Indeed, when they thought back about this summer, they agreed that it had been particularly exciting in a way they could not have anticipated on that first day when the classroom window splintered and the declaration of war landed at their feet.

The Three Weeks

The students of the Bnei Abraham Talmud Torah were deeply moved by Rabbi Greenberg's story of the tragic events that transpired during the Three Weeks — the siege of Jerusalem and its capture and destruction by the soldiers of Nebuchadnezzar, and once again many years later by Titus.

"Every year we recall these events," explained Rabbi Greenberg, "not only to be aware of our people's history, but also to learn a lesson which can be applied in the present time. By avoiding the transgressions which caused the destruction of the Bais HaMikdosh, and even more by learning Torah, observing the mitzvos, especially those of 'Gemilas Chasodim' and love of fellow Jews, we can hasten the redemption of the Jewish people and the rebuilding of the Bais HaMikdosh."

This thought struck Benny, the Talmid Chochom of the group. When classes were over, he walked home with Yossi. He told him, "I wonder whether there is something special we kids of B.A.T.T. could do during the summer to hasten the coming of Moshiach, besides fasting on the Seventeenth of Tamuz and the Ninth of Av."

"But," remarked Yossi, "how could anything we youngsters do have any influence on the rebuilding of the Bais

Hamikdosh and hasten the Redemption for which the Jews have fasted and prayed for two thousand years?"

"Don't say that," interrupted an unfamiliar voice behind the two boys. Benny and Yossi turned around to see who had so unexpectedly entered into their conversation. The voice belonged to a tall, stately man with a flowing, brown beard and a broad, black hat.

"Pardon me for breaking into your conversation. But I couldn't help overhearing what you two discussed as you walked in front of me. You reminded me of a story which is well-known to all young children of Jerusalem, from where I come. You know of the Kotel HaMaaravi, the Western Wall, the only part of the Holy Temple which still stands."

"Of course," replied the boys.

"Well, once a famous Rabbi spent the whole night of Tishah B'Av at the Wall, reciting Tehillim and crying over the destruction of Jerusalem. It was long past midnight when his eyes closed and he began to doze. Suddenly he heard a voice. 'Gamliel, Gamliel, why do you sit here and cry? Tears alone won't build Jerusalem. Deeds will!'

" 'What deeds?' asked the Rabbi.

"The voice replied, 'Every joy, every smile, in the heart of an orphan adds a stone to the walls of the future Bais HaMikdosh.'

"When the Rabbi awoke, he realized that it was only a dream. But a dream at the Kotel is more than just a dream. So the Rabbi took the words of the voice to heart, and he devoted the rest of his life to build and run a large Orphan Home in the Old City of Jerusalem, where the unfortunate children of Torah scholars who have passed away, would be well taken care of. Once a year, right after Tishah B'Av, the children of this large Orphan Home go to the Kotel. They spend the night there, reciting Tehillim, in gratitude for the event that gave them their beautiful home, where they get a good education and learn a trade."

"Does this home still exist?" Yossi inquired.

"Yes," replied the stranger from Jerusalem. "They had to move to a smaller place when the Arabs took their building in the Old City. They are in poor circumstances right now. I am sure they could use some good food packages and clothes, and maybe some books and tools for their workshops."

"Do you have the address?" asked Benny excitedly.

"Yes, my young friend. Here, I'll write it down for you. A pen-pal friendship with children your age there might be a good idea."

But Benny wanted much more than just a pen-pal friendship. The next afternoon, after classes at the Talmud Torah were over, Benny summoned all the children to their gathering place, the little wall behind the building. He related to them the story which the stranger from Jerusalem had told them. "I think here is a wonderful chance for us to do something constructive, in the spirit of the lesson of Tishah B'Av. It should be lots of fun, too."

"But how can we raise the money for packages and for tools and clothes?" asked little Shloimele who was of a very practical nature. "I don't think we should send old clothes, which people give away. If we want to make those unhappy children happy, we should give them something that is worthwhile sending."

Everyone agreed that Shloimele was quite right. Benny said, "Let's first write to the Home and find out exactly what things they need most. It doesn't all have to be done only during the Three Weeks. If necessary we can spend more time on this project."

All agreed that it would be advisable to get the information from the Orphan Home in Jerusalem, as Benny suggested. But, Yankel as usual, had some objections.

"I have no doubt," he said, "that the orphans in the Home in Jerusalem can use our help. But it seems to me, since we have only recently learned in the Shulchan Aruch (Code of Jewish Law) that the needs of the poor people in our own town take precedence over the needy in far-away places . . . If, as the story of that Rabbi goes, a smile on the face of an orphan adds a stone to the future Beis HaMikdash, I believe a smile on the face of the orphans right here, in our own city, will accomplish this just as well. We should rather visit the Jewish orphan homes here, in New York, and see what we can do to make things pleasant for them."

For a moment Benny was speechless. Most of the students of the Talmud Torah were swayed by Yankel's argument. But Yossi, his usual calm self, stood up slowly and said, "I think Yankel is right. Let's appoint him chairman of a committee that will visit the Jewish orphan homes here in our city and see what we can do for them. I am sure, though, that they have all the food they can possibly use, and also clothes, while the children in Israel need our help urgently."

Everyone was happy about this compromise of Yossi's. While Yankel was making plans for visiting Jewish orphan homes in New York, Benny wrote an air mail letter to the Home in Jerusalem.

Two weeks later a letter arrived with pictures of the Home and of the children and the exact information they wanted. The happy director of the Home thanked Benny, and several children wrote about their activities. Proudly, Benny read the Hebrew letters to the rest of the boys and translated it for the benefit of the younger ones who did not know enough Hebrew to understand its contents.

Rabbi Greenberg estimated that the items requested would cost about $500.00. But he suggested that some of the items could be obtained by soliciting from large Jewish manufacturing companies. Then the boys of B.A.T.T. really went to work.

The first request of the orphans was easiest to fulfill. Each of the boys chose a name on the list as a pen-pal. Raising money for food and clothing was obviously more difficult. One of the boys came up with the idea of challenging the students of the other Talmud Torah of Brooklyn to a tournament in various sports, and to charge admission. Someone else suggested that the tournament be not only in sports, but also include a contest in Hebrew, Chumash and Jewish History.

Soon letters went out to all the Talmud Torahs in Brooklyn. Seven of the larger schools accepted the challenge and gladly volunteered their help for this worthy project. Each Talmud Torah volunteered to sell a certain number of tickets for the big event.

On Sunday, the first day of the tournament, hundreds of friends, relatives and neighbors of the Talmud Torah students packed the seats of the Central High School Field. The local councilman threw out the first ball for the first baseball game between B.A.T.T. and Brownsville Maccabee Talmud Torah. Yossi proved to be the master pitcher not only of B.A.T.T. but of all the Talmud Torahs in Brooklyn. His curves,

sliders, and fastballs baffled the best sluggers of the Maccabees.
And Yankel laid down the bunt that advanced Benny from
second to third base, from where he stole home and earned
the run that gave B.A.T.T. the victory, and qualified them for
the finals.

One of the most memorable moments of the day was when
the tournament was stopped for a brief intermission and Benny
stepped up to the microphone to read the letter from one of the
youngsters of the Orphan Home in Jerusalem, and to explain
to the crowd the purpose of the special competition. He told
the people of the voice that the Rabbi had heard at the Kotel
HaMaaravi and of the decision of the boys of B.A.T.T. to institute during this summer a Gemilas Chesed Campaign to help
the unfortunate orphans of Jerusalem, and thereby expedite
the rebuilding of Jerusalem. When the students of the Talmud
Torah went around with baskets after Benny's speech, not a
single person in the large stadium of the high school field refused
to give a donation.

The next Sunday, the tournament continued, again to a
packed stadium and enthusiastic crowd. The B.A.T.T. team
did not win the basketball tournament. The team of the
Brighton Talmud Torah beat them, but only by one point,
with the crowds screaming their voices hoarse. B.A.T.T. did
win two relays and Benny and Roy Dorf placed first and
second in the Best of Ten Jewish History Questions Contest.

From the sale of the tickets and through the appeals made
by Benny, they made over six hundred dollars after all expenses
were deducted.

But that did not end the Three Weeks campaign. The
newspapers carried reports of the tournament and the charity
campaigns for both the local and the Jerusalem orphan homes.

A few days later, a letter arrived at the Talmud Torah, addressed to the Committee for the Orphan Home in Jerusalem, from a large tool company in Brooklyn. The company offered to ship, free of charge, all the necessary machines and tools for the shop of the Home in Jerusalem, as their donation to the Three Weeks' Project.

As a result of the newspaper publicity, a local radio station offered the boys of the Talmud Torah free time on the air to describe the various Jewish orphan homes in New York that they had visited and to solicit aid for toys, sports equipment, books and other needs of the children of the orphan homes.

That Tishah B'Av, when the boys of B.A.T.T. sat on the floor, as is the custom, to mourn for the destruction of the Bais HaMikdash, deep in their hearts they felt the joy of knowing that they had done more than just mourn. They knew that they had been actively involved in a project of "Gemilas Chesed," kindness to unfortunate Jewish children. And in this way, they were sure that they had helped to speed the coming of Moshiach and the rebuilding of Jerusalem in our days.

The New Super

The first time the hero of this story came to Bnei Abraham Talmud Torah, the boys almost burst out laughing at the sight of the grotesque, short, chubby man with his hat slightly askew at the back of his head. What made Reb Moishe Kaidanover look really funny was his outsized, bulbous, deep red nose, one side of which seemed pushed into his face. This deformity was the result of a vicious slash from the knife of a Nazi. But whoever got to really know Reb Moishe, as he was fondly called, became his friend and admirer. It was always a special treat when the strange looking Rabbi came every year in the fall to spend a week in the neighborhood as the personal guest of Rabbi Greenberg.

Rabbi Greenberg first met Rabbi Moishe Kaidanover when he, Rabbi Greenberg, was still studying for his "Semichah," Rabbinic ordination. He was deeply impressed by the scholarship of this odd-looking yet friendly man who, in his youth, studied in one of the famous Lithuanian Yeshivos. Reb Moishe's knowledge was phenomenal and his humility and ability to make friends with everyone, young or old, was even more overwhelming. He directed the American office of a Yeshivah and Kollel in Israel that subsisted on the funds Reb Moishe raised for them. He travelled from city to city for the institution, soliciting contributions. He used this opportunity to visit his many friends, telling them Torah stories, inspiring them with fascinating parables from the Dubner Maggid and Chassidic Rebbes. He was equally popular for the scores of songs and melodies he would sing and teach anyone, and for the inspiring way he would lead the prayer services in his beautiful tenor voice. His great scholarship and beautiful voice combined to make every "Seudoh Shlishis" or "Melave Malka" that he attended a source of deep joy and learning. Although he had suffered much in his personal life, losing his wife and son during World War II, he had the inner strength to overcome his grief by his great faith and his willingness to set his own feelings aside and comfort others.

The boys of B.A.T.T. were his fans, and waited anxiously for the week he would spend in their neighborhood. When he finally came, much of his time was spent talking to the boys, telling them stories about the scholars and sages of the Yeshivos of Eastern Europe, many of whom he had known personally. Occasionally, he would reminisce about the sad years when Hitler invaded Eastern Europe and destroyed the great centers of Jewish life, scholarship and culture. The only thing the boys could never get Reb Moishe to talk about was his personal tragedy. Rabbi Greenberg had told them that Reb Moishe had lost his entire family in an attack by Ukrainian collaborators with the Nazis on the hideout where a large group of Jews from Vilna had hidden in an abandoned mine shaft. Deftly, he would divert their attention by speaking about his experiences as a partisan — an underground guerilla fighting the Germans; how he was caught by the Germans several times and sent with thousands of others to the concentration camp but each time successfully jumped off the trains and escaped; how he and his friends the partisans had freed some of the trains by blowing up the railroad tracks or a bridge and overwhelming the guards.

When Reb Moishe was in the neighborhood, all the boys spent Shabbos at the Talmud Torah, enjoying the beautiful "Zemiros" (table songs), the inspiring prayers and fascinating stories. "Sholosh Seudos" lasted until dark and "Melavah Malka" way into the night. All the boys were inspired and uplifted by their being in Reb Moishe's company.

It is no wonder then that Reb Moishe was the favorite guest at B.A.T.T., and that all the students volunteered to help him raise funds for his Yeshivah and Kollel. Each afternoon of the week, a few of the boys went along with Reb Moishe to visit the old addresses and introduce him to new people from a list they compiled prior to his arrival. In fact, they had a contest going who could provide more addresses of homes which would take one of Reb Moishe's charity boxes.

One late afternoon, Benny, Shloimele and Roy Dorf accompanied Reb Moishe. The people in the area received the short, heavy-set scholar with the grotesque look like their own long lost friend and engaged him in discussion about their problems. He was welcome everywhere and got more donations than anyone might have expected in that neighborhood of not very affluent people, small businessmen, artisans or craftsmen who worked hard to make a living.

That day, something happened that turned this enjoyable experience into a most sensational event. As the boys were walking with Reb Moishe, he was telling a particularly fascinating story about the journey of the author of the "Shulchan Aruch," the Code of Jewish Law, Rabbi Joseph Caro, from Turkey to Safed in Israel. They were so engrossed in the story that they did not notice what was going on around them in this rather poor neighborhood where various ethnic immigrant groups lived. They were passing one of the large, grey apartment buildings that abounded in this area, when someone sitting at the entrance to the basement of the house began to call them offensive names. Had this come from some rough kids they would not have cared so much. But it was a bald man with an ugly, red face, wearing heavy overalls, sipping a can of beer, who hurled all kinds of vile insults like "dirty Jews," "lousy Jews," "cheaters," and similar invectives. Roy Dorf who was new in the area and had never heard such insults, wanted to return the insults. Reb Moishe held him back.

"If you don't respond to them, it upsets them even more. They love to get us all riled up. Just disregard the old drunk," he advised.

As they went on, the man cursed in Polish, "Zhidus, pshakrev Zhidus, Zhidus!" he yelled loud enough for even Reb Moishe to stop his story for a moment and listen to the voice. By that time, they had arrived at the little shop of an old tailor who was one of Reb Moishe's greatest admirers and never let him walk out without at least a five dollar donation, which in his situation was a large sum for he was quite poor. Once inside, they forgot about the insults hurled at them outside. This time Reb Moishe's visit was particularly welcome because the old man had just lost his wife, and he was very lonely and gloomy. Reb Moishe's cheerful and comforting talk made the old man feel much happier. Reb Moishe told him that his own wife and young son, after only three years of marriage, were brutally slaughtered by the Ukrainian collaborators with the Nazis, who were even more vicious and cruel than their masters, the Nazis.

Reb Moishe emptied the two charity boxes that were filled to the top with quarters.

"My wife used to put in a quarter every night before she went to bed," said the old tailor. "It gave her courage and faith to go on, even after her serious illness sapped her strength and endurance. I have kept up her custom since she passed away — may her kindly soul rest in peace."

"Wait a minute," added the tailor, as Reb Moishe and the boys turned to leave. "Here is fifty dollars my wife saved up for charity in the Holy Land. Take it for your Yeshivah in Eretz Yisroel and have one of the students say Kaddish for my wife's sainted soul."

They were all in good spirits when they left the shop. But as soon as they went out on the street, the growling, raspy voice of the man sitting in the basement entrance again began to fling insults at them.

"There is that nasty super again," said the tailor. "He is new around here. He is a drunkard and insults people, especially Jews. We have complained about him to the owners of the building but they say he is the best super they ever had; he is an excellent handyman. The Poles, Lithuanians, and Ukrainians who live around here like him because he speaks their language. We don't like this man because even our non-Jewish neighbors who tolerate the Jews begin to be influenced by him."

An especially vicious invective in Ukrainian pierced the late afternoon calm. It seemed to wipe away the cheerful look on the face of Reb Moishe. From the corner of his eye he suddenly perceived the ugly features of the old drunken super, and the sight hit him like a rock. He turned white; heavy beads of sweat broke out on his forehead, and his red, bulbous nose seemed to turn maroon.

"Yuvan, the terrible!" he screamed at the top of his voice. "Yuvan, Yuvan!"

He dropped his two heavy leather bags and with a speed that amazed the boys, he ran across the street, down the block to the apartment house, jumped the three steps down the basement entrance and threw himself upon the super who had half risen from his folding chair and flung the empty beer can into the face of Reb Moishe.

"Yuvan, Yuvan, where is my wife Zoshya, my little Yossele, Yuvan, Yuvan?" he moaned.

His fists flailing, Reb Moishe lashed out against the super who towered above the short, chubby Rabbi who had flung himself upon him, trying to choke him. His muscles bulging, his face covered with sweat and the foam of the beer, the super shook off Reb Moishe as if he were made of cotton, and began to punch him wildly and rip off his clothes. The three boys jumped in and tried to hold him down. Roy, a football player, threw himself on the super with a flying tackle and got him partially off Reb Moishe, whose face was bleeding heavily. But all three boys were no match for this violent, brutal creature with the muscles of a wrestler. Kicking viciously, he shook them off like little puppies, all the while using one hand to punch Reb Moishe, whose screams of "Yuvan, my poor Zoshya! Yossele!" filled the air.

From all sides people came running. When the super saw the gathering crowd and the approaching police cruiser, he turned and began to run, dragging Reb Moishe who was clinging to Yuvan's trousers, after him. Snarling, the super pulled out a long, sharp knife and was about to swing it at the bleeding, screaming Jew dragging after him, when two powerful policemen seized him. A third one had to help them subdue the violent, kicking super, who several times shook them off.

Reb Moishe was crying and sobbing, and bleeding profusely from the cuts on his face. The medics of an ambulance that had arrived on the scene gave him First Aid.

"Yuvan the terrible! That monster, was the leader of the Ukrainian auxiliary guards," he sobbed. "With his bare hands he would kill Jews! Nothing could stop him, not even bullets. It was as if the devil himself protected this evil, cursing, drunkard. It was he who discovered our hideout in the woods, while we were away on a mission of mercy, trying to stop a trainload of cattle cars filled with Jews from reaching its destination — the concentration camp Auschwitz. When we returned, we found one survivor — a child who had hidden deep in an old mine shaft. He could hardly speak. All he did was scream 'Yuvan, the terrible! Yuvan, Yuvan!' and place his hand around his neck like someone choking him. My wife and child were among the massacred. Since then, not a single night has passed that this nightmare of Yuvan has not haunted me — it stands before my eyes as he chokes my Zoshya and my little Yossele with his bare hands. How often have I heard his taunting 'Zhidus, pshakrev, Zhidus! Hep, hep, Zhidus.' We learned to disregard it, not to get angry and react. I don't know how many hundreds or thousands of Jewish lives he has on his conscience, if a monster like this ever has a conscience."

The police took Yuvan into custody and eventually he was brought to trial and punished for the war crimes he committed against the innocent Jews in Poland.

A Simchas Torah to Remember

The boys of the Bnei Abraham Talmud Torah always looked forward to Simchas Torah. Together with their teacher, Rabbi Greenberg, they sang and danced and showed that they understood the importance of this day when Jews complete the annual cycle of reading the Torah, only to begin over again. For weeks they saved money to buy soda, nuts, cake, fruit and candy for the Simchas Torah party to which they invited all the children of the Project and surrounding neighborhood. In this way they attracted many new students for the Talmud Torah and also had a wonderful time themselves.

On the first day of Sukkos, Benny and Yossi took a long walk through the neighborhood. It was one of the older sections of Brooklyn where once many thousands of Jews had lived, but had since moved away to better neighborhoods. But there were still Synagogues on practically every street of the crowded area. As it was around Minchah time, Benny and Yossi stepped into those Shuls that were open to see what was doing inside. They found mostly older people who were quite surprised to see the two boys in their Yarmulkas come in, look at the Seforim on the shelves, and ask questions about the young people and children of the congregation.

"You know what," Yossi said to his friend after they had visited a good many of these once beautiful but now mostly

111

empty Synagogues. "I pity the people in these Shuls. They don't have anyone to make it lively. It's all so quiet and serious. I wonder how they can really enjoy a holiday if they have no youngsters to celebrate with them."

"Wait a minute, Yossi. You just gave me a swell idea. Remember Rabbi Greenberg told us about the Chassidic Rebbe who sends his students to far away places to visit the Jews in their Shuls and to talk to them and share with them the joy of the Yom Tov. I think we students of B.A.T.T. could do the same thing in our own neighborhood. Imagine how lonely and sad it must be on Simchas Torah in these old Shuls that we have just seen. We are having all the fun and are really enjoying the happy holiday. How would it be if we spend part of our time making the rounds of these Synagogues and showing them some of the real spirit of the Bnei Abraham students?"

That was one of the most joyous Simchas Torah celebrations in the history of the entire neighborhood. For the boys of the Talmud Torah were not satisfied with visiting the Shuls individually. They organized a big parade of the children who had flocked to their party and as they went from one Synagogue to another, more people joined them to see what was going on. At first, they entered the Shuls hesitantly because they did not know how the people would receive them. But when they observed the faces of the old people light up with happiness at a sight they had not seen in their Shul for many years, the boys were encouraged to go on to the next Shul. They sang in the streets as they marched from one place to another. Even strangers who did not know what it was all about realized that this was a very happy occasion. For weeks and months the Jews in the Synagogues of the neighborhood spoke with admiration of the boys of B.A.T.T. who shared their own Simchas Torah joy with them.

But our story has another episode to it that made this Simchas Torah parade a very special event. Recently, two new boys who spoke only Yiddish, had joined the Talmud Torah. Their father died in a Nazi concentration camp and their mother had smuggled them out of Poland. With the help of a refugee organization, she came to the United States with the boys. Boruch Lefkovitz, a quiet, shy boy was the older one, and Menashe was his younger brother.

Rabbi Greenberg introduced them to his students on the first day they came to the Talmud Torah, and the boys of B.A.T.T. decided to do their very best to make these unfortunate orphans happy. They taught them how to play baseball, punchball, and all the other popular games; they invited them to their homes and birthday parties; and generally made a special effort to make them feel like part of the group.

The boys all tried to make them happy and at ease. But it seemed that all their kindness and helpfulness did not succeed in driving the sadness out of the big eyes of the two Lefkovitz brothers. Even when they were involved in fun activities, Boruch and Menashe still seemed unhappy. The memories of their father and an older brother who were killed by the Germans before their eyes, and of the other brutalities which they had witnessed, never seemed to leave them.

When the Simchas Torah party was in full swing at the Talmud Torah, Boruch remarked to Benny that his late father had taught them a beautiful song for Simchas Torah. Benny observed the sparkle in the eyes of the boy as he mentioned this song. At his suggestion, Rabbi Greenberg asked Boruch and Menashe to sing it for the crowd, and to the great surprise

of all the boys, who had never seen the two refugee children
saying more than a few words at a time, the two actually got
up and sang "Sisu Vesimchu" with a sweet voice. Somehow
they did not seem so unhappy after they sang their father's
song. The two boys also went along on the parade through
the neighborhood Shuls. And wherever the boys of B.A.T.T.
stopped to join the festivities in the Shuls, the Lefkovitz
brothers were asked to sing their father's song.

The happy Synagogue parade brought the students to one
large Shul where they found a score of old people who welcomed them eagerly. Among them was the venerable Rabbi
Yankel Goldstein, one of the patriarchs of the community, a
"Talmid Chochom" and a successful businessman, who, though
he could well afford it, had refused to leave the neighborhood
and the Synagogue where his old friends lived, prayed and
studied Torah with him.

All was happiness and joy when the youngsters from the
Talmud Torah, with their large following of friends and
observers, came to the Shul. In due course, Boruch and
Menashe were called upon to go up to the Bimah and sing
their beautiful song. Their sweet voices harmonized to the
soft but happy melody, and everyone, even the boys of the
Talmud Torah who had heard them sing it quite a few times
now, were touched by their inspired singing.

Rabbi Goldstein was among the crowd that gathered
around the Bimah when the boys from B.A.T.T. came in. He
missed the liveliness of youngsters in the Shul, especially since
his own children and grandchildren had moved away and came
to visit him only rarely. So the surprise visit brought back
memories and happiness which he not known for a long time.

When Boruch and Menashe came up to the Bimah to

sing, Rabbi Goldstein whispered to his neighbor, "You know, these two little youngsters look just like we used to look in our young days in the Old Country. They are real 'Cheder Yingelach'."

But when the two boys began their song, Reb Yankel looked startled and perturbed; his serene, patriarchal face grew paler than the white of his long beard. Excitedly he arose from his seat and stared at the two youngsters, his lips forming the words of the song along with them, and his fingers nervously tapping out the rhythm on the bannister leading up to the Bimah.

As usual, applause, "Bravo!" and "Wonderful!" filled the air. Reb Yankel pressed forward through the crowd up the stairs, seemingly in a trance.

"Let me up! Let me up! I must speak to these children," he begged.

"Who taught you this song?" he demanded of the bewildered boys.

"Our father sang it in Shul with us every Simchas Torah. His grandfather composed it and everyone knew it as 'Boruch's Sisu Vesimchu'," answered Boruch shyly.

With a moan, unable to speak, the old man threw himself over the two boys, embraced and hugged them.

"My sister's grandchildren. You must be my sister's *einiklach*. Thank the L-rd who had let me live to see someone alive of my family. I thought you were all dead, killed when the Nazis came into our town," he cried.

Over and over again he repeated those words. The two boys were astounded.

Reb Yankel explained, "I am your grandmother Shaindel's brother. Reb Boruch Lefkovitz was my sainted brother-in-law, and your father Yaakov was my beloved nephew. My children! My own sister's flesh and blood!"

After Yom Tov, Reb Yankel Goldstein rented an apartment for the boys and their mother, fixed it up for them most beautifully. He saw to it that they would have all the comforts they so richly deserved after so much suffering at the hands of the Nazis. And he derived much joy from the two children who grew up in the same spirit they had in the old home town in Poland.

The boys of B.A.T.T. often discussed the exciting climax of their Simchas Torah parade which had certainly given them more joy and fun than their usual celebration in the Talmud Torah building. They agreed with Rabbi Greenberg that it was truly an act of Providence. It was Hashem's reward for the good intentions of the boys to make others happy. For to make others happy, gives most happiness to oneself.

Purim at the Police Station

If you would have told the boys of B.A.T.T. that their grand scheme for a Purim project would end the way it did, they would have laughcd you right out of their meeting at the little wall where they always gathered after classes were over. They wore winter jackets, snow boots, shawls and fur hats, for this took place soon after Chanukah and the weatherman had predicted snow. But neither the prospect of snow nor the frosty late afternoon air could deter the boys from their outdoor meeting to discuss the most exciting event of their school year.

As always Benny came up with a suggestion that aroused the imagination of the boys, and at the same time made them feel warm inside. They did not care to have projects and parties like other boys in other neighborhood clubs or schools. Rabbi Greenberg had often told them that whatever they undertook should have some purpose. Even the happiest, most fun-filled project undertaken by boys who learn Torah must serve some good to someone, somewhere. Thus, all Bnei Abraham Talmud Torah affairs were so planned that they accomplished something positive, or served some good cause, in addition to having fun. The annual Purim project was no exception. There never was a question that the boys wanted a "Purim Shpiel," with loads of fun for themselves and for the audience who waited eagerly for this annual presentation of the Talmud Torah kids.

"I've had enough of the story of the Megillah," shouted Yossi heatedly, when the discussion centered around the "Purim Shpiel." He quickly corrected himself when he saw the raised eyebrows and heard the surprised, "What?" of his friends.

"Of course I don't mean that I have had enough of the story of the Megillah itself. But isn't it time that we do something different! Every year, again and again, we present Mordechai, Haman, and Esther in one form or another. Let's use our brains to think of a different idea for our 'Purim Shpiel.' One that will be entertaining and serve some meaningful purpose," he explained.

After much heated discussion, Jakie Segal, a new student, came up with a bright idea. "My uncle Joe is a junk dealer. He has a large, open truck. Cousin Elli, who drives it for his father, won't mind lending it to us for Purim afternoon, and he might even help us by driving us around the East Side, Williamsburg, Boro Park, Crown Heights and other Jewish neighborhoods."

"What do you mean, Jakie?"

"What do we need a truck for our 'Purim Shpiel.' You're crazy."

"You are out of your mind."

"Wait a minute, kids," said Shloimele, in his high pitched voice, quick to defend the new boy. "Let Jakie talk."

They calmed down long enough to give Jakie a chance to explain himself.

"You see, I was thinking about what Rabbi Greenberg

read to us yesterday about the great need of helping the religious Jewish farmers and settlements in Israel who observe Shmittoh — the Seventh or Sabbatical Year, when it is forbidden to plow, sow or work the fields. Remember, he explained to us that they could not plant anything and that it will take till next year's harvest until they can again live off the produce of their land. That is why the Rabbis of Eretz Yisroel appeal to us to help those who meticulously observe the laws of Shmittoh. Instead of the usual box collection, I thought, we ought to do something special this year for our brothers who will get little help from those who do not know or do not care about Shmittoh. While you were speaking about a Purim project, the idea came to me that this would be an excellent opportunity for us to really do something valuable if we could come up with a scheme that would raise big money. Here, in our poor neighborhood, we can expect to raise only a meager sum. But if we could perform our 'Purim Shpiel' in the wealthier neighborhoods where Jews celebrate Purim, I bet we could raise a large enough sum of money. That's where the idea of my uncle's truck comes in."

The response of the boys was loud and enthusiastic. "Great!" "Fantastic!" "Good show, Jakie!"

But then Yankel, the pessimist of the group chimed in. "Naturally, you are all in the clouds about this hare-brained scheme of Jakie. Have you perhaps given some thought to what you can do on a truck, what kind of 'Purim Shpiel' can you perform that will attract the crowds on the street, and make them open their wallets and pocketbooks?"

They hadn't really though of that. What could you do on a truck, without so much as a stage?

But Yossi, brainy Yossi, came to the support of his new

friend's idea. "Naturally, Yankel, you must always spoil our
fun with your doubts and pooh poohs. I think Jakie's idea
is wonderful. I know his Uncle Joe's truck. It's old and kind
of shaky. When Cousin Elli rides it hard through the streets
it shakes and rattles all over, like a mighty Purim 'Gragger.'
But it certainly is as wide as any stage we've ever acted on.
We can attach curtains on the large poles that stick out on
both sides, and put on a real show."

"I have a good suggestion, I think," piped up Mordechai,
the boy from Israel who had recently come into the neighborhood. "I play the accordion, and I know lots of Purim songs
from Israel."

"Wonderful, Mordechai," applauded the boys, now getting
really excited as the plans began to take shape.

"My brother and I play the Chalil," said Yitzi, not willing to
be outshone by Mordechai and his accordian.

"And we can all sing Hebrew songs together, in Purim
Shpieler disguise. With Berel's guitar and David's drums, we'll
have a real band to lead us," chimed in Ephy.

On Purim, which that year fell on a Sunday, the boys
of B.A.T.T. met very early in the morning. A committee of
"handymen" fixed up the sturdy, old junk truck into a majestic
"Shushan Playhouse on Wheels." Even Uncle Joe would not
have recognized it after the boys got through decorating it with
streamers, posters, a curtain and all the trimmings of a stage.
Cousin Elli, who graciously volunteered his services to drive
the truck, got into the spirit and put on a Haman uniform.
Yossi's job was to set up a loudspeaker and to act as announcer.
The play itself was especially prepared and rehearsed by Benny.

The first performance took place in front of the Talmud

Torah in their own neighborhood. Everything went just swell. Rabbi Greenberg was very proud of his boys, as he watched them perform on the truck stage, and especially when Yossi told of the plight of the needy religious farmers in Israel for whom the proceeds of this "Purim Shpiel" were to go.

Mordechai, the accordianist, surprised everybody by the way he handled the large instrument which he had brought with him from the Holy Land. Supported by Berel and David, his lively music and the joyful singing brought much applause and helped make the "Purim Shpiel on Wheels" a real success. Then, when the boys went around with their charity boxes, everybody dropped in some coins. Some were so impressed by the enthusiasm and sincerity of the Talmud Torah students that they even put in dollar bills.

"Look, boys," said Benny, after completing the first successful performance. "I suggest we go right down to the East Side now. There is always a huge crowd on Delancey Street on Sunday. There we can draw a large audience and then we can go to Crown Heights and Boro Park."

So a few minutes after the applause had died down, the truck, guided by Elli's skilled hand, rattled across the Williamsburg Bridge.

"Hey! Over there on the corner of Delancey and Norfolk Streets, where Delancey Street becomes wide, is a good spot. We are in nobody's way. Let's stop here and put on our next performance," said Yossi.

Yossi's keen eye had spotted a perfect location. They parked the truck at the curb. Mordecai's accordion led the B.A.T.T. band in a rousing performance of "Shoshanas Yaakov," which even the Delancey Street crowd, which is used to all kind of far-out ideas, shenanigans and sidewalk performances, took proper note of. Cousin Elli parked right in front of a large Jewish restaurant. And when Yossi spoke his "spiel" into the loudspeaker, his announcement of a free performance of the "Purim Shpiel on Wheels," a large crowd gathered. Everything was just perfect. The lively crowd of old and young, in the happy Purim spirit, applauded enthusiastically, clapped and sang along with the B.A.T.T. Band. Then the large Pushkes were passed around, and just like on their home ground, the people of Delancey Street, inspired by the lusty performance of the boys and Yossi's appeal for the farmers of Israel who observe Shmittah, opened their pockets wide and gave generously.

Just as they were about to wind up the collection, as Mordechai was leading the band into one of his liveliest songs to keep the crowd in a joyous spirit, they heard the wail of a police siren. A group of policemen pushed through the crowd. The boys realized then that they had put on their performance right around the corner from a police station. They did not imagine that there was anything wrong with their free Show on Wheels until the police lieutenant demanded that all the collection boxes be handed over to him. With tears in their eyes, the boys relinquished the heavy large cannisters that were filled to the top with coins.

"Who is in charge?" he asked Elli, who was sitting at the wheel.

"Benny, back there in the costume of Mordechai," he answered.

Still wearing his long, black beard, Benny stepped forward, and the mumbling and increasingly loud protests of the crowd began to make this into a public incident which attracted an even larger crowd.

"Did you get a permit to put on a performance here or to make a street collection?" the officer demanded.

"Well, well, well . . ." stuttered Benny. "I did not know that this was necessary on Purim."

"What do you mean on Purim! A law is a law on any day. All of you boys follow me."

He signalled Elli to start the truck and the police car sounded its siren to force a path through the huge crowd that was getting angry and threatening the police officers. Then Mordechai had an inspiration. He let go full force with his accordian and the B.A.T.T. Band and the whole huge crowd began to sing "Utza Etza" as they followed the police cruiser to the Norfolk Street Stationhouse.

It was probably the liveliest parade in the history of Delancey Street, if not of New York, as the police car led the truck with the Bnei Abraham Talmud Torah Purim "Shpielers" and Band and the admiring crowd from Norfolk Street to Clinton Street and into the big yard of the gloomy old police headquarters. The whole atmosphere changed from an unpleasant incident which had threatened to get out of hand, into a real Purim mood.

The police captain in charge could not hide his smile when the parade entered the yard, with the boys in their costumes and Mordechai pumping his instrument, followed by the singing crowd.

"What's this all about?" asked the captain, after he was finally able to get something resembling quiet.

Benny explained the situation and pleaded, "We didn't know it was against the law. We just thought of the needy people in the Holy Land, and of the people around here, whom we can give a happy hour in the spirit of Purim. That's why we put on this Show on Wheels."

The captain considered this for a moment. Then he said, "But ignorance is no excuse."

Just then Sam Blau, the councilman who lived on Grand Street, walked in. "Come on Cap," he said. "Give the kids a break. They mean well. And the money is going for a good cause. I'll arrange for a retroactive permit."

"Yes, give them a break," shouted those of the crowd who were able to press into the yard.

"Okay, boys. Since this is Purim, I am giving you a chance. On one condition," the Captain agreed.

For a moment the boys, whose hearts had been lifted by the pleas in their favor and the friendly smile on the Captain's face got frightened. The fenced in jail windows looked down at them rather menacingly.

"The condition is that you put on another good performance for my men right here in the yard, and for those jail birds who are looking down at you from those windows."

The thundering applause of the crowd was mighty. And the performance of the boys was every bit as stirring as the preceding ones, perhaps even a bit more. For they had experienced something of a little miracle of their own. The police officers, too, appreciated the fun and opened their own wallets to contribute to the boys' collection.

Needless to say, the "Purim Shpiel on Wheels" was performed several more times after the Hon. Sam Blau got them an official permit. Next stop was Eastern Parkway. And from there, 13th Avenue in Boro Park, where they performed before the happy crowds.

Even happier were the boys when they got together in the Talmud Torah the next day, opened their collection boxes, and counted out close to four hundred dollars, to be sent to Israel by Rabbi Greenberg.

"We certainly won't forget this Purim and its exciting experiences," they all agreed.

It had been a most unusual and very rewarding day for them. It left them with an especially good feeling, because in addition to their own fun and excitement, they had helped an important cause in Israel and made friends for Torah Yiddishkeit in New York.

The Return of Itzy

One day, Melly Schreiber, the former leader of the Cellar Rats, who came back to B.A.T.T. after the boys saved his life from the hands of hoodlums, came running over to his classmates shouting, "Hey! Did you see the announcement of a basketball championship for the Talmud Torah and Hebrew Schools of Greater New York? The winning team will compete in the city wide Day School Athletic League championship. Every Borough champion will get a library of books of Hebrew and Jewish content for their schools. We have a beautiful library building, but not enough books. How about it?" he ended breathlessly.

"Aw, we don't have big, tall guys, and few of us play basketball anyway. We don't even have a decent basket. The one on any garage door is better than the old iron hoop we use here," Yankie, the usual critic, objected.

"Well," said Yossi, "Roy and I have already been discussing that we should practice more basketball; it's becoming the most popular sport, and Jewish players are among the best right here in City College and in other schools."

Roy Dorf chimed in, "As far as height is concerned, the best players are not necessarily the giants. They are the fast, smart guys who have a good hand and sharp eyesight. Most college teams have only one or two very tall men who can dump the ball into the basket. The regular team guys are just average height. And, besides, I don't think the other Hebrew Schools and Talmud Torah have bigger guys than Sammy and Melly."

"What do you mean, Yankie? Why you've got a great hook-shot and you can needle the ball right into the basket from twenty-five feet away. I saw you do it last night in my backyard. That's worth three other guys!" David said.

All eyes looked to Benny whose word carried most weight among them because of his great popularity and his reputation as the best student of B.A.T.T.

"Well, I don't know if we can field a team good enough to win a library. But I think that by participating in the tournament we could perhaps do a lot of good, perhaps even a real Kiddush Hashem. And that's even more important. Perhaps, if we boys whose interests lie more in the study of Torah and the observance of mitzvos can successfully compete with others whose minds and interests are more on sports and similar things than on their Hebrew studies, it may have a good effect on them and on their parents who will be watching the games. But let's get Rabbi Greenberg's approval first. He might object if it takes too much of our time."

Rabbi Greenberg thought that the idea was a good one, as long as the boys limited their training to the hours after classes and Sunday afternoons. And since it was always one of his hopes to have the money to set up an extensive library, the chance of winning one, as slim as it seemed, was attractive.

Melly was selected captain of the team. He went to Mac Dunn, Big Mac, as everybody called the athletic director of the neighborhood youth center, for advice. Melly knew him from the days when his Cellar Rats had practiced handball and shooting baskets at the Center. Big Mac offered all kinds of suggestions for organizing the team and came over to the B.A.T.T. playground to help Melly lay out and paint the courts. He gave the boys an old time clock, other old or spare equipment, and manuals with the official rules and instructions. He even got permission for the B.A.T.T. team to use the indoor court of the Center during the long "Motzei Shabbos" evenings. The P.T.A. of B.A.T.T. volunteered to provide the boys with uniforms for the competition.

Soon Melly had mustered enough boys from the two oldest classes for a first and second team. Sammy, the oldest and tallest, and Melly were the best to work under the basket. Yankie, Yossi and Roy Dorf were excellent in the center. Jake Siegal was very good at blocking. And surprisingly enough, "shortie" Shloimele was so fast, short and skinny that he could slip past the best defense or block of the other side. Melly spent much time with him to overcome his lack of technique in handling the ball with his short, weak arms. By the end of the winter, the boys could practice on their own playground. The team was good enough to play regular games on Sunday afternoons, and devise all kinds of plays and strategies suited to their particular needs and talents.

One Sunday afternoon, early in March, as Melly was running his teams through their drills, a hoarse voice began to heckle them from the other side of the fence.

"You guys stink! Why don't you learn how to shoot?" and similar nasty comments.

But the boys of B.A.T.T. had long ago learned to disregard any taunting from the sidelines.

"Hey, Melly, why don't you teach those punks to dribble and handle the ball right," shouted the heckler, loud and clear through the crisp March air. "You oughta know better!"

Angrily, Melly turned around to tell the heckler to be quiet. He took a quick look at the lanky guy in the ragged clothes, his sailor cap pulled low onto his forehead, his mouth with many of its teeth missing, open, and yelled in recognition.

"Itzy, Itzy Weiss, the skunk from Maujer Street! I don't believe it. When did they let you out and back down to this turf?"

While the boys took a break and watched interestedly from afar, Melly walked over to the boy leaning against the fence, put his hand through and grasped his hand.

"Take over, Yankie," Melly called. "No time to waste."

"How did you get in with these yarmulke punks, Melly, you the boss of the Cellar Rats?" asked Itzy.

"Well, Itzy, these boys saved my life when I was about to be cut up by Muggie, the big hood, for the same reason that he and his gangsters managed to pin the rap on you and have you sent up the Hudson to do time. I've come back to school and Talmud Torah. I wish I had never left it. I learned my lesson. What about you, Itzy? I still remember your Dad. He was so proud of you. 'Itzy Weiss is going to be a big man in the Golden Land with his brains and sense,' he used to say."

"Yeah. He was a good man who worked hard all his life as a presser in a coat factory. It broke his heart when he saw me quit school and run around with the pack. He had a heart attack when they caught me with the stuff that Muggie and the hoods had pushed on us. He died two weeks ago. That's why they let me out on probation sooner. My mother and kid-sister have no one to take care of them. I've got a lot to make up to them for what I did to my old man. Meanwhile I am back in the old Maujer Street Shul, saying Kaddish in the morning and evening, feeling awfully guilty. Up at the place, they taught me how to handle tools and work with motors. If I can get a job in a garage or a machine shop, I might go back to night school and do all the things that would have made my Dad proud of me. He blamed himself for always being so strict with me and expecting so much from me."

"Melly, Melly, we need you," Yankie called. "Come on, Mel."

Melly signalled to the boys that he'd be right there.

"Sorry, old pay, I kinda liked your Dad. Too bad a man like him had to work so hard. He helped us in our school work and knew history and math so well. He was real religious too. For his sake, Itzy, stay away from the old gang and hangouts. I'll help you if I can."

Itzy who had been staring into the air, pulling his sailor cap even lower down on to his face, pushed it back up, looked at Melly, and said, "Say, Melly. How would you like it if I were to coach your basketball team?"

When Itzy saw Melly's hesitancy, he pulled a black yarmulkeh out of his pocket. "Ask the old Shammes in the Maujer Street Shul — remember how he used to chase us when we gave him trouble? Ask him how serious I've become. I haven't missed a single service since I came back."

Melly still wasn't sure it was a good idea having a boy like Itzy around B.A.T.T. "I know, Itzy, you were the best shooter and blocker in the group who played basketball at the Youth Center. You could help us a lot. But, look at these

kids. Now look at yourself in the mirror . . . I had a tough
enough time getting back in the groove here, and I was a student
here only two years before. But you . . .!"

Melly looked at the unhappy fellow, the cigarette butt
dangling from the corner of his mouth, his eyes shaded by the
sailor cap.

"You know what, Itz. Let's go speak to Rabbi Greenberg.
If he agrees to your idea then it's surely okay with me. But
get rid of the butt."

Rabbi Greenberg greeted Itzy Weiss in a very friendly
manner. But when Melly told him the purpose of Itzy's coming,
Rabbi Greenberg was skeptical about letting such a fellow —
with such an appearance, and especially such a background —
come in close contact with his beloved students.

"I know how you feel," sighed Itzy. "And I understand
it better than anyone else, Rabbi. But this morning after I
finished saying Kaddish for my father, who was a real Talmid
Chochom, who ate his heart out because he was forced by
circumstances to be just a presser of coat collars, and could
not afford to sit and learn all day, and to give me and my
kid sister a proper Jewish education, and who died of a broken
heart because I, who he thought would make his own dreams
come true, ended where I did — this morning, Rabbi, believe
me, I decided to turn a new leaf. I want my Dad's soul to be
proud of me. And I want to make up to my mother and sister
for the shame and sorrow I caused them. I think being with you
and your boys, even if only as the basketball coach, can help
set me straight. If only I could find a job and get back to night
school."

While Itzy waited outside, Rabbi Greenberg and Melly

talked it over. "Recently, when we were learning about Teshuvah (Repentence), you explained to us the importance of helping someone who is down and out find his way back. It's even more important than giving charity," pleaded Melly.

"I know, I know. And I appreciate how you feel, Mel. But my first concern must be for the boys, for you, for your parents. How can we be sure he doesn't fall back in with some of his old pals, revert to his old ways and get into trouble."

"Rebbi, I know the boys' welfare is more important than that of just one boy, especially someone like me or Itzy. You took a chance on me. I hope I haven't disappointed you. And if Itz doesn't find a job, he'll be forced to go back to his gang."

"Wait, a minute. Maybe Joe McGinness, the mechanic who repairs my car, would take a boy like Itzy as an apprentice, if I recommend him. He is a tough boss, but he is a decent and good man. Let me call him."

A few minutes later, Itzy was on his way to Joe McGinness' shop.

Joe shook his head dubiously when he saw the tall, lanky kid in the jersey and sailor cap walking in diffidently. "Let me see how you handle tools," he said.

It didn't take Itzy long to convince Joe that he would make an excellent apprentice. "Just remember, no nonsense here or you are out on your ears. If not for Rabbi Greenberg, you wouldn't have a chance."

That's how the basketball team of B.A.T.T. got a coach, a talented one, who knew all about strategy, and could teach the boys the techniques of dribbling, shooting and blocking like real pros. Itzy was there every Sunday afternoon and twice during the week for a practice session and individual work outs.

"Itzy, you are a magician. You oughta go into this professionally. I bet you there are plenty of schools that would use a guy who can do for their team what you have been doing for us," Melly complimented him. The boys were enthusiastic about having a coach like Itzy and learned quickly.

Mac Dunn came by one day as Itzy was working with some boys under the basket at the far end of the court. He was greatly impressed with what he saw. He watched them practice and said to Melly, "It's incredible how your boys have improved since I last saw them. I don't know about the other Hebrew School League teams and how well they play, but you really look terrific. Even if you don't win, you'll certainly put up a good show."

He watched the team for a while longer, then asked, "By the way, Mel, who is that big guy there coaching your boys? He sure knows what he is doing."

"Would you like to meet him?" asked Melly, and signalled Itzy to come over.

Big Mac's eyes opened wide and his mouth fell open.

"What . . . this fellow?" he gasped.

Itzy, suddenly stopped short in his nonchalant walk from the other side of the court as he recognized Mac. He stared a second, turned and ran; one big step up the fence and a jump over. A second later he was out of sight, leaving everyone surprised and bewildered — everyone except Big Mac.

"Hmm. I thought I'd recognize him again if I ever came face to face with him. I've something to settle with him . . . "

Melly told him that Itzy Weiss had changed, that he had turned a new leaf. He related how Joe McGinness was very satisfied with his apprentice, as he told Rabbi Greenberg whenever he came to him for service, and how the old Shammes of the Maujer Street Shul, and especially poor Mrs. Weiss were so overjoyed with the "new" Itzy. "It would indeed be sad if all this were to end now."

"I sympathize with all that, but what made him run off so fast is too serious to just forget about it. Sooner or later it will catch up with him, regardless how much he changed."

Itzy disappeared without a trace. Search as they might, the boys of B.A.T.T. couldn't locate their missing coach anywhere. It wasn't only the basketball tournament that they worried about. The Shammas of the Maujer Street Shul had phoned Rabbi Greenberg that Itzy hadn't been back to Shul to say Kaddish and to study with him.

Joe McGinness was angry, too. "Here, we give a guy who is down a fair chance," he complained. "He was doing real well — a handy guy with tools and motors. I'd bet he would end up an engineer with a good career ahead of him, and he jumps off just like that, without saying a word."

And worst of all, Mrs. Weiss was unconsolable. Rabbi Greenberg and Benny went to visit her. "He was so good that I wished more than ever that my poor husband was still alive to see his Itzy go straight. He earned enough to keep us well supplied with food. He went to Shul regularly, and Friday night was a real Shabbos again in the house, with candles and all," Mrs. Weiss sobbed. "He came rushing home one evening, packed a few things, and said, 'Mom, don't worry, I'll be back soon. I have to clear up something first'."

The time for the basketball tournament was approaching. Before May 31st, the neighborhood champ had to be chosen. And the first Sunday in June was to be the Brooklyn Boro Championship game in the outdoor courts of Prospect Park. The finals were scheduled for a week later, at Yeshiva Center in Manhattan.

Melly, Yossi and Benny were sitting on the little wall behind the Talmud Torah, watching the game of their two teams.

"The teams are in excellent shape; Itzy has done a marvelous job, teaching them the fine points and strategies of the game," said Benny.

"But the zest is missing. We'll never get as far as the Boro Championship without Itzy," commented Yossi, who was resting his left leg that gave him trouble if he strained it too much.

"Nothing new, yet, no clues, no leads, Mel?" asked Benny.

Melly shook his head sadly. Suddenly his eyes lit up. He exclaimed, "Why didn't I think of Tommy before. How could I forget Itzy's pal, the big Irish kid. Brain and Brawn they used to call those two in school. Perhaps he can help us. I know where he lives."

Tommy McLaughlin's family lived in the drab area of light industry in Greenpoint. His father worked in the metal factory on the next block. Melly and Benny went to look for Tommy.

They reached the neighborhood and Melly recognized Tommy's house by the big hoop at the wall where the Cellar Rats used to practice basketball at night, under the street lamps.

They rang the bell. The door oepned, and out came an older, heavy-set worker in his undershirt and pants, his muscles bulging.

"Get outa here, you Jew boys," he shouted when he saw the boys with the yarmulkehs. "I am fed up with you. Ever since that Itzy got hold of my Tommy he has been in trouble. Finally, Tommy had come around, was working on a decent job, there comes that guy again and we haven't seen Tommy since. Get away from here!" And he shut the door in their face.

They turned away gloomily. But from the front yard of a neighborhood house, a woman walked with them for a few steps.

"Don't mind my husband. He has good reason to be angry; but it's not your fault. I just want to let you know that Tommy has been in touch with me. He assured me that he and Itzy are well and are trying to clear up something."

They went home, a little more at ease in their hearts about their coach.

The preliminary games were on and Itzy was still nowhere to be found, nor was he heard from. The boys from B.A.T.T. did well, and reached the Boro Championship game in Prospect Park. Everyone began calling them the Tzaddikim because their "tzitzis" were hanging out from under their dark blue jerseys with the two white Luchos (Tablets) on the back. They almost lost this crucial game when Roy Dorf's yarmulkeh flew off because a player from the Brighton Talmud Torah pulled at it in an attempt to stop Roy from shooting. But he caught it in time with one hand while sinking the basket with the other after a high leap into the air.

When Melly and Yossi saw their opponents, the Little

Davids, from the Etz Chaim Hebrew School of Bensonhurst, in their red jerseys with the Magen David on their backs, they were depressed.

"We're no match for these big guys with their brutal force and unusual height. They'll run us off the court," said Melly.

It seemed that Melly's words would come true a few minutes before the end of the game. All the boys and many of the parents from both Hebrew Schools were gathered around the outdoor court in Prospect Park. The B.A.T.T. team, which consisted of Melly, the captain, Yossi, Roy, Sammy, the only one who could match the Little Davids in height, and Yankie, backed up by Benny, Jake and Shloimele —their secret weapon — was fast enough, and had learned Itzy's lessons of strategy and handling the ball so well that for a while they were able to balance their opponents' strength. They were leading Etz Chaim by six points going into the third quarter. But it soon became obvious that the greater strength of the taller Little Davids would prevail. Yossi's left foot acted up when he tried to cover too much ground, and he had to be taken out. Neither Benny, nor Jake, had the same capacity to keep the ball moving as quickly as Yossi.

By the time the fourth quarter started, the B.A.T.T. team was exhausted. But a few words of encouragement by Rabbi Greenberg breathed new life into them. They went in and played with the last ounce of their strength and pulled even. But a few second later, the big boys in their red jerseys, dumped several baskets over the heads of their smaller opponents. The clock was moving fast. Melly kept changing the players to give them a few minutes of rest. Six more minutes, indicated the clock. Yossi came in again, also Roy, who had been kicked in the stomach in the third quarter. Big Jake Siegel, his arms high in the air, caught whatever came his way. The Little Davids were ahead by three points and seemed to control the court as the B.A.T.T. boys got more out of breath — their most effective weapon, their speed, gone. Suddenly, a whistle blew a signal.

"Itzy! Itzy!" cheered the boys as the tall, lanky boy in the dark blue Jersey with his tzitzis flying high in the air ran alongside the court whistling signals. There it was, the daring strategy that no one but he could think up and use.

"Go Shloimeleh, go, go," yelled the kids from B.A.T.T. The bigger boys had made room for their little star to come from behind and run right through the middle of the field and in between the big bruisers in the red uniforms, catching them by surprise, as Sammy and Jake had feigned backwards and pretended to move up along the left side of the court.

Yankie was up front, ready for the ball, when Shloimeleh came close enough. Yankie dumped the ball into the basket just at the moment one of the tallest Little Davids pushed him with his elbow. The foul was enough for the B.A.T.T. team to score and pull even.

"Itzy, Itzy," yelled the whole crew from B.A.T.T., when he gave the signal to Melly to follow through with one of his long distance throws, and Melly needled it straight into the basket for the win, just as the whistle of the referee blew.

They wanted to carry Itzy on their shoulders around the court in triumph, but he said, "Wait a minute, boys. First I have to talk to Rabbi Greenberg. I owe him and you an explanation."

While the crowd was waiting to cheer the victorious team, his friends who were close enough to Itzy, listened with excitement as he told Rabbi Greenberg how he and Tommy had been used by Muggie's hoods to keep Big Mac busy at the youth center one evening just before he closed up. While they were arguing with him, refusing to leave the court where they were practicing, Muggie's boys broke in downstairs, stole much of the equipment, busted the cashbox and took the money.

"Tommy and I were suspected as accomplices. Unless we could bring some evidence or get the other guys to admit that they had done it without our knowledge, we could be brought to trial for it. When Big Mac saw me, there was just no other way but to get out, go after the other guys, and persuade them one way or another to clear our names. It took a lot of doing, Rabbi Greenberg. And it broke my heart to disappoint you, my mother, Joe McGinness in the garage, and most of all, my young pals here.

"I'm so glad I came back just in time. And believe me, Rebbi" — everyone realized that it had special meaning when he said "Rebbi" — "this was the final chapter of my life in the 'street.' I have learnt my lesson. Now I can do what I promised myself that day in the Maujer Street Shul, after saying Kaddish."

Needless to say, all was joy and exultation at B.A.T.T. for the next week. Itzy took extra time and effort to polish the technique of his team. The final game was attended by Hebrew School kids and their parents from all over the City. Many had heard and read about the incredible Tzaddikim from B.A.T.T., and many had come to show their support and root for the boys in their flying "tzitzis."

No, the B.A.T.T. team did not win. The team from the Midtown Hebrew Center was simply too strong and had too much skill. B.A.T.T. lost in the last two minutes by three points. But they gained the respect of the hundreds of Jewish parents and students who saw them play. And Itzy, Melly, the captain, and the young team were the heroes and the talk of all the Hebrew Schools. Rabbi Greenberg happily accepted the certificate that entitled Bnei Abraham Talmud Torah to purchase a thousand dollars worth of books of Jewish content.

The Threshold's Secret

The two shiny silver-grey buses pulled out of the school yard of Bnei Abraham Talmud Torah early in the morning for the annual Lag B'Omer trip. Berel with his guitar, was in a really good mood, and under his leadership there was lots of singing on the trip along the Hudson River on the beautiful spring day. They stopped at several lookout points to admire the scenery, take pictures, and move around a bit. Their plan was to follow the river all the way up to the Bear Mountain Bridge and then to turn left into the mountains, find a suitable spot near one of the lakes and eat lunch. There they were to set out on a hike across Torne Mountain, take a ride on the Trail Cable Tramway and meet the buses again further up near Fort Montgomery. They divided into three groups, each equipped with a trail map of the Palisades Interstate Park.

Everything went smoothly. They stopped for lunch near Brook Lake. From there several trails led northeast around Mt. Torne. The younger boys, led by Rabbi Greenberg and Yankie, took the tramway trip across the ridges, mountains and valleys. From the top they were to go south towards the Queensboro Furnace Ruins and wait for the two other groups, one led by Sammy and Yossi, and the other by Benny.

The boys were well-prepared with knapsacks, heavy shoes,

sweaters, plenty of food, small Siddurim, cups for washing the hands, and a small shovel.

Yossi and Sammy followed the trail to the right of the mountain. Benny's group turned to the left, the shorter but steeper route. It was real good exercise and Benny's boys made excellent time, following the markers and stopping only briefly every half-hour. The stronger boys helped the weaker ones up some of the steep inclines, hoisting each other up or supporting each other up the rocky cliffs. They reached their destination by five minutes before three, the time they had set for themselves to link up with Yossi's group. They were all excited and happy, but very tired, and were glad to settle down on the beautiful spot near the recreation area from where they could see anyone approach from any side.

At first, they were not concerned when Yossi's group did not arrive on time.

"One can never tell following mountain trails what comes up," Faivel remarked. He was among the more experienced climbers in the group, having been a scout and spent a whole summer in Bear Mountains at camp.

Yet, when the clock pointed to four o'clock and there was no sign or signal from the other group, Benny became worried. In just one hour they were to meet Rabbi Greenberg and the buses at the Queensboro Lake which was some distance away. Melly, second in command to Benny, took most of the boys to meet Rabbi Greenberg and to inform him of the delay. Benny and three of the strongest boys, Faivel among them, set out on the trail on which Yossi's group was to have followed around three o'clock. They left word of their destination at the desk of the recreation area. One of the park inspectors called all stations to find out if there had been any report of an emergency. There were no such reports and none of the other groups that had come up the trail in the last few hours reported anything unusual on the trail. Benny was to call from one of the trail phones if he found that he needed help.

Well, the kind of help that was needed was not the kind that the park and trail attendant could give. Benny and the three boys were only half way down the steep inclines when they saw three members of Yossi's group, led by Sammy, rushing up the trail.

From afar, Benny shouted, "Hey boys, what's the matter? Quick, what happened?"

It took Sammy a few moments to catch his breath; then it came out in spurts and bursts.

"Yossi sent us ahead. We got into some trouble . . . We stopped at an old country store for some refreshments . . . One of the boys was going down the steps from the side entrance when he saw Hebrew words on one of the steps . . . He called us. The stone that served as a doorstep must have come from a Synagogue and it has a "Sheim," the name of G-d, engraved on it . . . Now Yossi is trying to convince the owner to let us remove it . . . But he is very stubborn . . . He says he found the stone there and does not think it is anyone's business if he leaves it there and people step on it. Whoever does not like it, does not have to come to the store."

"Let's not waste any time, Sammy. Take us there so that we can phone Rabbi Greenberg and the park attendant at the summit that we are all right and there's no cause for worry. And we shall see what we can do about the desecration of the Sacred Name of G-d."

At the end of the trail in the valley, they turned into a

country road and soon arrived at the country store — and not a moment too soon. The owner of the store had called the state police when he became annoyed by the boys' persistence.

"If you don't clear out of here in five minutes, we'll take you to the stationhouse and keep you there until your parents come to get you. That will teach you not to annoy people," threatened a tall, burly police officer.

"Wait a minute, sir," Benny said bravely, "I am the leader of this group and I can take care of them. They do not want to do anything wrong. They are merely trying to do what their religion teaches them to. They are not out to bother anyone."

"Why," broke in the store owner, "Who do you think you are to tell me what to do? In your place you can do what you want. Out here, in my store, I am the boss; no one is going to force me to do anything I don't want to do. Officer, there has been enough talk. Get rid of these pests or else I'll take care of them myself."

"Sir, we are willing to pay whatever it costs to have this stone removed and your entire staircase rebuilt," Benny tried again.

But the old man just stood there, his face burning with anger, shaking his fist at the boys. "Get out of here before I take my whip to you."

"Enough of this nonsense," said the tall officer, pointing to Yossi and Benny. "You two come with me. The rest of you continue on your way. We'll see what the justice of the peace has to say about your disturbing a law abiding citizen."

"Gladly, officer," Benny replied. "We'll go with you and

see if the Judge can do something to help us. You boys meanwhile continue on your way to meet Rabbi Greenberg and then join us at the police station."

A few minutes later, the state troopers drove Benny and Yossi to the police headquarters. Their worried friends hurried up the trail, and from there to the meeting point to inform Rabbi Greenberg of the latest disturbing development.

Although the two boys pretended to be unperturbed, they were quite concerned. But their fear was somewhat allayed when they saw the old man with the wrinkled face and white hair, before whom the officer took them. They had done nothing wrong, but it would take an understanding judge to help them. And this man looked like he would!

Yossi related their discovery of the doorstep that must have been a head-stone over the door of a Synagogue. Benny explained that if people were permitted to step on it the name of G-d would thereby be desecrated.

"Your Honor," he said, "We offered to pay the cost of replacing this stone with a brand new one, but the owner would not hear of it."

"Wait a minute, boys. You just reminded me of something." The judge called the officer over and whispered something in his ear.

Soon the officer came back with an old man.

"Levi Green, tell me, whatever happened to the old Synagogue over there in Rockland County; I remember a case a good many years ago against Rocky Burkom, the storekeeper."

"Your honor, this is like opening old wounds. I was the last member of the old Congregation. All the others have died or moved away. Why bother again, even though the old rogue does not deserve it," he said sadly.

"Well, Levi," explained the Judge, "These boys got into trouble with Rocky over something that might interest you. Listen to their story."

When Benny related the incident, Levi got red with anger.

"The old crook," he shouted. "Bad enough he foreclosed the mortgage on my Uncle Jacob and took his business away; he even dragged away the stones from the old Synagogue in revenge. He had no right to do that."

"I thought so," remarked the Judge dryly. "It's just like Rocky to do such a nasty thing. Too bad we did not catch him that time when he destroyed all the documents that would prove that your uncle, not he, owned the land where the railroad built the track. Your uncle trusted him too much and taught him all he knew about the business. Then he turned around and cheated him."

The boys did not quite understand what was going on. But a minute later, Levi Green filled in the details of the story.

"My Uncle, Jacob Green, who had been a peddler, bought large tracts of land in the valley where he speculated that the New York Central would build the new railroad. The railroad company changed their plans and moved further northwest in Rockland County. Most of the Jews who lived here followed the line. My uncle, who invested most of his money in this venture and even put a high mortgage on his home and the store which he had built behind the old Synagogue, was in lots of financial trouble. The old crook, Rocky, had been his assistant. He'd driven the horse and buggy for my uncle and learned the trade from him. In his dismay over the failure of his gamble, my uncle wrote some of his land over to his assistant, as if in payment of a debt that really never existed and dated it back so that his debtors should not be able to take it away. He made Rocky sign a paper that he was to return it after the trouble would be over. Soon afterwards, my uncle died of a stroke. Somehow Rocky got hold of this paper and destroyed it. There was no way of proving that the land did not belong to him and that my uncle did not really owe him money. He claimed that the land was not worth enough to cover the 'debt,' so he took away my uncle's house and store too. Everyone in the valley knew it was a crooked deal, but nothing could be done. The written agreement could not be found. My aunt was left with nothing and she moved to her children in New York. The old Synagogue gradually fell apart after it had been emptied of all the Seforim and other religious articles by the members who moved away. Now the old crook has used some of its stones for his store. Maybe he thought that if people stepped on the Hebrew inscription, they would wipe out the memory of his deception and stop calling it Uncle Jacob's place . . ."

The boys were deeply moved by this sad story, but the Judge brightened their mood when he said, "At any rate, there is a good chance for you boys to get the Synagogue stone in Rocky's stairway. Here is a warrant granted to Levi Green, the only member left of the old congregation, to reclaim the stone. Be here again next week, on Wednesday afternoon at 3:00 P.M. If Rocky Burkom has not delivered the headstone of the Synagogue to this court by then, we'll prosecute him to the full extent of the law."

During the entire trip back to New York, and for the rest of the week, the boys were discussing their discovery and the sad story connected with it.

The following Wednesday, Rabbi Greenberg, Benny and Yossi drove out to the valley at the outskirts of the Bear Mountains, where Levi Green met them with a smile.

"You boys don't know what you have started. Just wait and see," he told them happily.

There was a large crowd milling about the small police court when they arrived. When the State Police had asked Rocky Burkom to give up the stone, he adamantly refused, and lifted his fists to strike the police officers. They had to restrain him by force. When they lifted out the stone, Rocky had tried to tear himself away from the state troopers and jump at the workers who had pulled out the stone. Underneath, they found a large yellow envelope. The judge was going to open it now. The boys were extremely excited. Levi Green introduced them to his relatives from New York, the sons of Jacob Green who were well-to-do businessmen, owners of a large clothing store in Brooklyn. They had been notified to appear in case they were needed to testify.

The Judge rapped his gavel on the desk, and the crowd in the small room, in the hall, and outside in the yard, came to order. He gave the background of the incident, of Rocky's refusal to permit the boys to purchase and replace the doorstep from his store at their expense because by the laws of the Jewish faith it was sacrilege to let people step on the Hebrew name of G-d. Then he explained the sequence of events that took place after the boys had been brought before him.

While everyone watched expectantly, he opened the sealed envelope that had been found under the stone. There was a large, faded, sheet of paper in it. The Judge held it up and read it slowly, shaking his head.

"Well, I kind of suspected it. Here is the document Rocky thought he had hidden forever. Here it is, signed and sealed by both Jacob Green and Rocky Burkom, proving that there was no real debt, that Rocky was to give the land back, after the trouble passed. What do you propose to do now, Rocky? The land is clearly not yours!" the Judge asked.

"I admit it all . . . I'll return everything. Just don't put me behind bars. I am too old," the storekeeper shouted hoarsely, his face pale as a sheet.

"Are you satisfied, or do you want to pursue the matter further?" the Judge asked Jacob Green's sons. "It is your right to bring this rogue before a court for fraud."

The two sons whispered to each other for a few moments. Then the older one replied seriously, "This crook, who repaid kindness with ingratitude, really does not deserve to be let off the hook. Yet, we are too old to enter into lengthy litigation. Let the thief return the property which he stole and repair the Synagogue which he desecrated. Let the rest be up to his conscience and G-d."

The large crowd applauded. They clapped even more, when the man continued, "I further would like to say that my brother and I, who, thank G-d, are in comfortable financial circumstances, agree that half of the money that we will earn from the sale of the property we will donate to the school of the boys who discovered the sacrilege. I have spoken to their Rabbi and he told us that they would like to build a new wing to their building for a library. There should be enough money in this to pay for the cost of the construction."

Thus it came about that during the next summer, the Jacob Green Library was added to the Bnei Abraham Talmud

Torah building. And the stone, which they had discovered on the threshold of the country store, was placed next to the entrance in a conspicuous place, in memory of the old Synagogue in Rockland County. A bronze tablet told its strange history, how it had come to be misused and how it had been salvaged and brought to this place of honor, in recognition of the boys' share in its recovery.

Mishmar Night Rescue

It was late one Thursday night when Yossi caught sight of the time on Benny's watch.

"Hey, Benny, it's past eleven. Time to break it up and go home, or else we won't be worth anything in school tomorrow. I wish, though, I'd really understand this point of argument between Rovo and Abbaye better. It's just the kind of thing Rabbi Shatzky may ask when he gives us the entrance exam next week."

"Don't worry, Yoss. On the way home I'll go over it again with you. You'll be accepted, I'm willing to bet," said Benny.

"Yeah, but in what class are they going to put me? Together with younger kids?" worried Yossi.

"Aw, come on Yossi. I know you haven't learnt Gemoro as long as most of us. But you have made up for it. Let's go home now. And stop worrying."

Ever since the boys had spent a few days at the big Yeshiva, they had plunged even more enthusiastically into their learning, as Rabbi Greenberg had hoped when he sent his best seniors there. The first thing they did was to institute "Mishmar" night, reviewing their week's learning on Thursday evening until 9:30. This time, they learnt even later. For Benny and Yossi were scheduled to take their entrance exam for the Yeshiva the following week. Benny was sure to get in. When they let the boys sit in on a "Shiur" (lecture) in the Yeshiva, he fitted into the class like one who had gone to a Yeshiva all his life. But Yossi, who had come so much later to B.A.T.T., was worried that he might not make it. So Benny spent a lot of time with him, coaching him, making sure that he knew everything inside out.

All the other boys had left the Talmud Torah at 9:30, after Maariv. Even Rabbi Greenberg had gone home, knowing that he could trust the two boys who continued to review the Gemoro in the brightly lit study hall of B.A.T.T. to lock up properly. The time just seemed to fly, when they realized how late it was.

Quickly, the boys closed the windows, turned off the lights, locked the doors, and walked out into the breezy spring night. Once again Benny was going over the difference of opinion in the Gemoro as they walked through the empty streets that echoed each footstep and the sound of their voices.

Benny suddenly stopped. "Say, do you smell something, Yossi?"

Yossi sniffed the cool air. "I think you are right. It does smell like smoke. There must be a fire somewhere around here!"

They checked the houses and rooftops of the long row of houses on both sides of the street. At the end of the block, in an old apartment house at the corner, they noticed something.

"Isn't that smoke coming out of the window near the roof?"

"Yeah. Isn't that where we delivered food packages for the poor, old, sick people before Pesach?"

"You might be right, Yossi. I just hope it's not their apartment that's on fire. The man is in a wheel chair and the woman hobbles around with a cane. Gosh! Yossi, run back to the Talmud Torah building. There is a fire alarm box right in front. Meanwhile, I'll run to the house, wake up the people, and see what else I can do to help."

Yossi was the fastest runner at B.A.T.T., but never in his whole life did he run as fast as he did that Thursday, racing through the empty streets to the building they had just left a while ago. He thought his lungs would burst. But he got there, broke the window of the alarm box with the attached hammer, and pulled the lever.

It took only a few minutes for the first fire engine to race up the empty street to the corner from where Yossi was calling. But watching billows of smoke mixed with tongues of fire stabbing the moonlit sky, he was unable to hold himself back, and he ran off mumbling, "They can't possibly miss the fire."

When he reached the apartment house, he saw Benny leaning out of the window on the top floor, yelling for help. Yossi climbed to the window of the ground floor apartment, held on to a narrow ledge and inched his way across until he reached the fire escape ladder on the first floor. He swung himself up, in his best gym manner, and raced up the narrow metal stairs — second floor, third, fourth. Down below people began to gather, screaming. The fire engine raced up, filling the streeet with ladders and hoses. Flames engulfed the roof of the apartment house. Yossi saw Benny holding up the old woman at the window with one hand, while grabbing for something inside with his other hand.

"Hold on, Benny! Hold on!" he shouted. Just as he was turning with his last ounce of strength from the platform on the floor below, he heard the faint cry of a small child. He looked down. Ladders were going up all over. The big red pump car was beginning to pour streams of water against the building. Though he wanted to move up one more floor to help his friend, he pushed the window in with his elbows. He crawled inside, holding his handkerchief in front of his face, as he had been taught in his First Aid course.

To Benny, at the window, it seemed like an eternity. The flames were singeing his face, arms and clothes. His grip on the old woman was loosening. His breath was coming shorter and shorter. When the first fireman reached him and took him into his strong arms, he was just about to pass out.

"Yossi, where is Yossi," was all he could whisper, pointing below.

"Don'tcha worry, kiddo. We'll take care of him too," said the fireman as he passed the unconscious boy down the ladder, while streams of water poured into the house from all sides.

The next thing Benny remembered was waking up in the hospital, his arms heavily bandaged. His parents and Rabbi Greenberg were sitting beside his bed. Flashbulbs were going off and reporters were shooting questions at him. He related to the visitors about the late study session in the Talmud Torah, and of their noticing the fire on the way home. Suddenly he remembered and stopped in the middle of the sentence. "Where is Yossi?" he asked.

When no reply was forthcoming immediately, he turned

to Rabbi Greenberg, pleading, "Rebbi, where is Yossi? He climbed into a window on the floor below me. Tell me the truth, please. Rebbi, what happened to him?"

"Don't worry, Benny. Yossi will be all right. He is downstairs in the operating room. He broke both his legs and one arm when he jumped a full floor down to the next landing with a baby in his arms. The doctors tell me that he will be fine. He was not seriously hurt other than the broken bones. And the baby is fine, too, they say," Rabbi Greenberg assured him.

Benny was home in a few days, returning to a hero's welcome from his neighbors who had read the newspaper reports of how he had dragged the two old people to the window and held on for dear life until the firemen reached him, as the fire began to burn the clothes and skin off his body. After a week's recuperation, Benny was able to leave the house and visit Yossi who was still in the hospital. It was quite a shock to see his best friend all bandaged up, both feet and right arm in casts. All Benny could see of his friend was his pale face.

A weak smile greeted him. With his one uninjured hand, he showed Benny a letter from the Yeshiva to which they had applied, welcoming him even without an entrance examination.

"We have read of your 'Mishmar' night experience and of your brave action. We will be proud to have you among our students," wrote the Dean of the Yeshiva. Benny could not be happier. He had received a similar letter, but he had never had any doubts that he would make it anyway. Surely, this piece of good news would speed Yossi's recovery.

"You should see the headlines you made in the News and the Post," Benny told Yossi. "Even the N.Y. Times had your picture and a full report about your heroic act of saving an infant from certain death. How did you do it?"

"The flames were coming at us from all sides. I grabbed

the baby out of her crib, ran out of the hall, and when the stairs collapsed, I jumped down to the next landing, shouting 'Shema Yisroel' from the bottom of my heart, worrying only about the baby, not my own life."

"What a great Mitzvah!" exclaimed Benny. "You remember what we learned, 'He who saves a single soul is as if he saved a whole world.' And you really did it! Wow!"

"But who is going to take care of her, Benny," asked Yossi.

"I heard that the little girl has a grandmother on a farm in the Midwest. She flew here to take the child and will raise her on the farm. She will have someone to give her love and whatever she needs."

It took quite a few weeks until Yossi was able to get around on crutches and attend the celebration in honor of their heroic deed. People kept writing and sending all kinds of gifts to the boys and to their Talmud Torah. Letters from the President of the United States, from the Governor, from the Mayor of New York, and from many other famous people became part of Benny's and Yossi's scrapbooks, together with the newspaper reports and pictures. But the happiest day for the two came in the fall when they both entered the Yeshiva. Yossi was still limping and some of the scars would always remain to remind him of the excitement of that Mishmar night experience.

When they asked Yossi to say a few words at the celebration in his and Benny's honor, he said humbly, "Divine Providence wanted us to be there, in time. So, I had some difficulty understanding Abbaye and Rovo. Now I have a chance to really learn and understand and to prepare myself to take on the challenge of what Divine Providence has in store for me to become a better Jew and human being."